RAG SOUP

an Emmett Love Novel - Volume 5

John Locke

TELEMACHUS PRESS

This book is a work of fiction. Names, characters, places and incidents are either the product of the author's imagination or are used fictitiously. Any resemblance to actual persons, living or dead, or to actual events or locales is entirely coincidental.

RAG SOUP

The publisher does not have any control over and does not assume any responsibility for author or third-party websites or their content.

Cover Designed by: Telemachus Press, LLC
Copyright © Shutterstock/217402621

Visit the author's website:
http://www.donovancreed.com

Published by: Telemachus Press, LLC
http://www.telemachuspress.com

ISBN 978-1-942899-06-8 (eBook)
ISBN 978-1-942899-07-5 (Paperback)

Version 2015.02.23

Printed in the United States of America

10 9 8 7 6 5 4 3 2 1

Personal Message from John Locke:

I LOVE WRITING books! But what I love even more is hearing from readers. If you enjoyed this or any of my other books it would mean the world to me if you'd take a moment to send a short email to introduce yourself and say hi.

I personally respond to my readers.

I would also love to put you on my mailing list so you can receive savings of up to 67% on eBooks immediately after publication. You'll also receive updates and have an opportunity to participate in contests and drawings.

Please visit my website,
http://www.DonovanCreed.com,
so I can personally thank you for trying my books.

John Locke

New York Times Best Selling Author

8th Member of the Kindle Million Sales Club
(which includes James Patterson, George R.R. Martin, and Lee Child)

John Locke had 4 of the top 10 eBooks on
Amazon/Kindle at the same time, including #1 and #2!

...Had 6 of the top 20 books <u>at the same time</u>!

...Had 8 books in the top 43 <u>at the same time</u>!

...Has written 27 books in five years in <u>six separate genres</u>,
<u>All best-sellers</u>!

...Has been published throughout the world in numerous languages
by the world's most prestigious publishing houses!

...Winner, Second Act Magazine's Story of the Year!

...Named by Time Magazine as one of the "Stars of the DIY-
Publishing Era"

Wall Street Journal: "John Locke (is) transforming
the 'book' business"

Donovan Creed Series:

Lethal People
Lethal Experiment
Saving Rachel
Now & Then
Wish List
A Girl Like You
Vegas Moon
The Love You Crave
Maybe
Callie's Last Dance
Because We Can!
This Means War!

Emmett Love Series:

Follow the Stone
Don't Poke the Bear
Emmett & Gentry
Goodbye, Enorma
Rag Soup

Dani Ripper Series:

Call Me
Promise You Won't Tell?
Teacher, Teacher

Dr. Gideon Box Series:

Bad Doctor
Box
Outside the Box

Other:

Kill Jill
Casting Call

Young Adult

A Kiss for Luck (Kindle Only)

Non-Fiction:

How I Sold 1 Million eBooks in 5 Months!

For Emmett, and all who strive to do their best;
For Gentry, and all who keep the home fires burning;
For Shrug, and all who live with disabilities;
For Penelope, and all who yearn for love;
For Hopeful Harold, and all who just want to get laid:
Bless you all!

RAG

SOUP

CHAPTER 1

PRAIRIE WOMEN ARE a sharp-tongued lot.

If you ain't been around 'em much, you might wonder how a wife might come to yell at you like it's your fault her stove broke 'cause she was cookin' your dinner at the time. Or how if some strange giant bug shows up on the floor you ain't never seen, it's on you to know what it is and how it got there. And God help you if she said "Kill it!" and you didn't know that meant get it out of the house first!

I still get surprised by my Gentry's moods, but I liken 'em to the weather: ever-changin', and apt to come at you from a clear blue sky, for no apparent reason. And when they hit, they're relentless, and overpowerin'. When I'm dealin' with Gentry or a thunderhead, best thing to do is find shelter, and weather the storm.

I'm tellin' all this 'cause she's been hollerin' at me non-stop for five minutes, ever since I made the mistake of tellin'

1

her the new school marm slapped our daughter, Scarlett Rose, across the face this mornin'.

Scarlett's almost five.

"You stand there and calmly tell me our daughter was *slapped?*" Gentry says, madder than a frost-bit mule. "In *public?*"

"That's my understandin'," I say, hat in hand.

What type of school teacher slaps little children?"

"Why, *all* of 'em, far as I know."

"Are you *insane?*"

I might be, I don't know. She's asked me more than once, so I reckon it's possible. She sees me glancin' at the bedroom door.

"Who are you looking for? Scarlett? *She's* not the one who hired a violent teacher."

I decide not to tell her I'm seekin' shelter, nor why. And anyway, she just said somethin' I didn't catch, but it ended with: "*You* hired her!"

"I did," I admit.

"Are you going to answer me?"

"About what?"

"What possessed you to hire a child-beating *she*-devil?"

"My understandin' is she *slapped* Scarlett."

"What?"

"She didn't *beat* her, she slapped her."

Gentry's face is three colors of red and about to explode. In times like these I always hope she remembers how much she loves me before she starts in, but in my experience it don't work that way. In that regard prairie women are more like fires than storms, 'cause a bad storm will quickly give way to nice weather, while a woman's temper–like a prairie fire–requires time and effort to put out. And when you finally get it under control, there's a whole lot of char to deal with 'fore things go back to normal.

She says, "What did you say to her?"

"The school marm?"

"No. Humpty Dumpty!"

"*Huh?*"

She rolls her eyes. "Yes, Emmett. The school marm. What did you say to her when she informed you she struck our child?"

"I apologized and said I'd have a talk with Scarlett."

"You *what?*"

I know from experience she don't expect me to repeat what I just said. What she means is...well, I ain't quite sure what she means. But it's clear whatever I *should* a' done with regard to the school marm ain't the same as what I *did*. And when she tells me what I should a' done, I nearly fall over.

"You should've slapped her back!" she says.

"Her *back?*"

"No, chucklehead! Her face!"

I'm tryin' not to look confused, but I know it ain't workin', 'cause Gentry's gettin' madder by the minute. She says, "Two weeks ago you shot a newspaper reporter in the hand for *talking* to Scarlett. But when your precious school marm *slaps* her, you just stand there and *apologize?*"

I ain't sure what the reporter has to do with the school marm, or why the school marm is suddenly mine, and precious, but I decide not to ask till I'm convinced the fire's completely out. In the meantime I say, "I'm sorry I handled things so poorly. But I hope you don't expect me to slap Miss Gilmore every time she punishes a child."

She takes a long minute to think on that, and the more she thinks, the calmer she gets. When her face is down to just two shades she asks the very same question I asked Miss Gilmore right off: "What did Scarlett do?"

CHAPTER 2

OLD TIMERS SWEAR it used to get so hot in Kansas they had to collect the eggs before dawn to keep 'em from burstin' into flames in the henhouse. They'll tell you times were so hard the worms used to pull the chickens right into the ground. And who ain't met the old timer that swears he had to stand tall and carry a stick in the winter to take a piss, 'cause the piss would freeze and he'd have to knock it loose with the stick?

I grew up respectin' my elders, and was taught to take their words to heart, but some a' these stories are harder to swallow than Shrug's rag soup.

First of all, who don't know it takes a Kansas hen twenty-five hours to lay an egg? What I'm sayin', if your hen lays at seven this mornin', she'll give her next one at eight tomorrow, which means over the next three weeks half her eggs'll show up after dawn no matter *how* hot it gets.

Second, in my experience, Kansas weather's generally pleasant, but given to extremes that range from winters so cold you could fall out of bed and break your pajamas, to summers so hot you'd be tempted to light a fire, hopin' to cool things off.

Of course you've got your twisters.

Kansas twisters are another thing altogether.

If you ain't from Kansas you'll underestimate 'em the first time. When you see 'em comin' your way in pairs or triples, you'll probably waste time marvelin' while the other town folk are runnin' around, tyin' themselves to somethin' sturdy.

But you'll learn.

I've lived through days so hot my piss wouldn't puddle, and nights so cold my canteen water froze, but I still ain't had to take a stick to my piss stream, nor seen eggs burst into flames. For one thing, if piss froze to your pecker it'd hurt like hell to bust it off with a stick. For another, if all them afternoon eggs was burstin' into flames, what kept the henhouses from burnin' down? Scarce as wood is in Kansas, if henhouses had *ever* burned down in mass quantities I expect some enterprisin' Eastern businessman would a' seen an opportunity to start a business to replace 'em. But I ain't never heard of a henhouse-buildin' business here or anywhere else.

On the subject of tall-tale tellers, there ain't many old timers left in Kansas these days, thanks to the war, Indians, bandits, cholera, typhoid, scarlet fever, consumption, pneumonia, brain fever, infections, diarrhea, and yes, extreme weather—it ain't a place where old folks flourish.

The reason I'm thinkin' about tall tales is related to the reason Miss Gilmore slapped Scarlett. Here's how I put it to Gentry: "Scarlett's been tellin' the school kids how they're gonna die, and when, and Miss Gilmore told her to stop tellin' tall tales."

"And she hit her?"

"Not right then. The hittin' came after Scarlett said the next part."

Gentry frowns. "So tell it."

"Word-for-word?"

"Yes, of course."

"Scarlett said Miss Gilmore was gonna die on a Tuesday after gettin' snake-bit in a shithouse on a Sunday."

Gentry's face clouds up again, only this time it's her that's lookin' at the bedroom door. "*Scarlett?*" she yells. "Get out here this *instant!*"

CHAPTER 3

I FEEL BAD turnin' Gentry's temper onto Scarlett, but it winds up bein' a good thing 'cause after givin' her a proper scoldin', Gentry calms down enough to remember somethin' she'd been wantin' to tell me. "Oh!" she says.

I look up from the salt block I'm grindin', and notice her eyes have turned bright and excited, the way I love 'em. Then she says, "Have you met our newest visitor?"

I wrap up the salt block, put it away. "Who we talkin' about?"

"John Boone."

"Nope."

"Well, you just *have* to!"

"Why's that?"

"Because you'll never guess what he does for a living!"

I sigh. If Gentry says I'll never guess, she's probably right. "I have no idea. What does he do?"

"You can't give up that quickly! I'm not ready to tell you yet."

"Then why'd you bring it up?"

"Because I want you to guess! I'll give you a hint: it's good for Dodge."

I frown. I hate guessin' a man's occupation even more than I hate guessin' if his dog's gonna bite. But since Gentry's in a good mood about it, I take my hat off to help me think better.

"Well?" she says.

"Give me a sec."

I want to say he's a preacher, 'cause that's somethin' the town really needs. We had Reverend Murphy, but he moved back to his boyhood home in Springfield after hearin' his entire family died. With a million ways to die in the West, it ain't uncommon for an entire family to be called to their maker overnight. But some deaths are stranger than others, and Reverend Murphy's might be the strangest of all, since his family was killed by their dinner table.

You might wonder how a dinner table could kill a family, and I'll tell you in a little bit, but right now Gentry's waitin' on me to guess what kind a' man has shown up that'd be good for Dodge. The reason I know he can't be a preacher is Gentry's met him and I ain't, and I'm the sheriff, which means Mr. Boone's first stop in town must've been the *Lucky Spur*, the bar and whorehouse Gentry and I own that she operates. In my experience a man who comes to town and visits a whorehouse first ain't likely to be a preacher. Nor is Gentry particularly fond of preachers, since they usually rail against whores, gamblin', and drinkin', which is our livelihood.

"Buffalo hunter?" I say.

"No, Emmett."

"Ranch hand?"

She shakes her head. "Bigger."

"Politician?"

She frowns.

I say, "Give me another hint."

"When word gets out what he does it could double the population of Dodge in six months!"

"Damn!"

"What's wrong? Why are you frowning?"

"'Cause I hate losin' business more than I hate guessin' games."

"Why would you lose business to a dentist?"

"Dentist?"

"What did you think I meant?"

"I figured he was plannin' to put in a whorehouse."

"You think I'd be this excited over a competitor?"

She's right. I hadn't factored in her excitement, even though I removed my hat. I take a minute to glare at it before sayin', "There ain't a dentist within 100 miles!"

"That's my point! We need to make sure he settles here. We could build him a shop, and make signs and put them up along the Santa Fe Trail to let the settlers know we not only have a sheriff and doctor, but a dentist, too! Folks will line up for a dentist!"

"Why?"

Gentry gives me a look like I'm as dumb as buttons on a dishrag. "You have any idea how many people suffer toothaches?"

"Most do, I s'pect."

"Did you know that four of every hundred people die from pains in their teeth when there's no dentist around?"

"I s'pect them figures come from the new dentist."

She frowns.

"Was he drinkin' or whorin'?" I ask.

"What difference does it make?"

"Just curious."

"Both."

"Can't fault him for that, I guess. Did he say where's he from?"

"What difference does *that* make?"

"I reckon I ought to travel to wherever he's from before we start advertisin' his abilities."

"Why?"

"Maybe he got run out of town."

"*What?* Who'd run a *dentist* out of town?"

"*I* would, if it kept him from gettin' killed."

She gives me a look of exasperation. "Emmett, what in Sam Hill is wrong with you? Why are you being so suspicious? Who'd want kill a *dentist?*"

"*I* might, if he was a danger to the town."

"That's ridiculous."

I decide to hold my tongue on the matter, since my experience with dentists is the complete opposite of Gentry's, and since I can't imagine *anyone* wantin' to be anywhere *near* a town that has one, let alone features him on signs. Sure, I could tell her about the two dentists I know of who got shot to death for the pain they inflicted on women and children, and the third who got hanged for killin' his patient, but that might lead to an argument, and what good ever come from arguin' with the person you love most in the world? I put my hat back on and decide to have a talk with this liquor-and-whore-lovin' dentist before Gentry starts letterin' signs about him.

I say, "You're right, Gentry. I shouldn't judge the man till I know him better."

Her face softens. "I didn't mean to sharp-tongue you, Emmett. I imagine being suspicious is a good quality for sheriffs to have. But you're a good man, and I know I can count on you to give him a proper welcome."

I ask how long till dinner's ready.

She smiles. "Is that all you ever think about? My biscuits and meat stew?"

I smile back. "Much as I love them things, that ain't what comes to mind first when I think of you."

"I know that look," she says, but her smile fades when she sees our neighbors walkin' past our house, headed toward town. She says, "If Enorma asks about my derringer, tell her it's broken."

"Is it?"

"No, but her moon-eyed husband might question you about it."

"She wants him to buy your derringer?"

"That's right."

I frown. "You sure about that? I mean, why not ask for a brand new gun? And why yours?"

"I expect it would delight her to shoot me with my own gun."

"Enorma ain't even fifteen yet. She's just a silly girl who admires you."

Gentry shakes her head like I'm the dumbest clod in the field. "You of all people should know that with the exception of my tits, Enorma Suiters wants everything I have: my gun, my clothes, my friendship with Rose, my child, my saloon, my husband...."

I know better than to go down that path, so I simply say, "She's our neighbor."

"Don't get me started on how you allowed *that* to happen."

Good point, since *that* particular discussion has led to many a cold night. "What'd you tell her was wrong with your derringer?"

"I said it won't shoot."

"That's it?"

"It was more conversation than she deserved."

I pause a few minutes to let her simmer down. Then say, "I know it vexes you I sold Ben Suiters the lot next to us. But I had no idea he was engaged to Enorma at the time. She weren't even livin' here."

"I know. But it's just awful for me. Not to mention all the other women in town who keep trying to woo you."

"Well, I s'pect every man in the county would give up an arm and leg for one of *your* kisses," I say.

"Men know better than to flirt with Emmett Love's wife," she says.

"Except for Harold."

Gentry lowers her eyes and smiles softly. "Hopeful Harold?" she says. "Why, that poor man was in his late nineties."

"Maybe so, but that never stopped him from askin' you for a poke. He even asked *me* if he could poke you!"

Gentry nods toward Scarlett, to remind me she's sittin' at the table and shouldn't be exposed to talk of men who want to poke her ma.

I agree, but Scarlett ain't payin' a lick of attention to us, so I ain't too chastened over it.

Hopeful Harold was 96 when he fell in love with Gentry back in the days when she was whorin' in Rolla, Missouri. He constantly tried to buy a poke off her, but she kept refusin', fearin' the effort might kill him. He said she could check with his doctor, and one day she did, and the doctor agreed she was right. He told Gentry that Harold's heart wouldn't be able to survive the activity, but he also said that Harold's dreams of bein' with Gentry was the only thing keepin' him alive, so he urged her to be kind to him and give him hope that someday she just might give him that poke. So every day Harold showed up at the whore house to ask Gentry for a poke and without fail she'd smile, kiss his cheek, and say, "Not today, Harold." He'd say, "What about tomorrow?" and she'd wink and say, "Ask me then, my darling, 'cause you never know."

No matter how bad things were in Gentry's life, she always greeted him with a smile and sent him away with hope, and that's how he came to be known as Hopeful Harold.

Unfortunately for Harold, I met Gentry and took her away from that life. I ran into him our last night in Rolla, and he had the gall to walk right up and ask me if he could give Gentry a poke before we left. I hadn't heard the story about him and Gentry, so I told him he was lucky he was in his nineties, or I'd have taken him to task. He said, "It'd be worth whatever you do to me if I could poke Gentry just once before dyin'."

I had to admire his grit, but told him it'd be a cold day before I ever let that happen.

When Harold heard that me and Gentry went to Springfield, he sold his house and made that perilous journey only to find we'd continued on to Dodge City. That was the year of the severe draught, and he couldn't find anyone to help him make the trip. Then the war broke out, and he got stuck in Springfield. From time to time he sent word to Gentry that he was still holdin' out hope for a poke, and every time she heard that it made her smile. Earlier this year she was pourin' whiskey for a man who said he was from Springfield. She asked if he knew Harold, and he said Harold died.

Oh, my goodness did she ever cry!

Though she barely knew Hopeful Harold, the news of his death set her to cryin' for two straight days.

And several times since then.

For her, losin' old, Hopeful Harold was like losin' a loved one.

We eat in general silence till Gentry looks up from her plate and says, "It'll feel odd eatin' dinner without Scarlett, don't you think?"

"She's right here," I say. Then answer Gentry's puzzled look by sayin', "It just seems strange to talk about her like she ain't sittin' right here at the dinner table."

"I only said it that way because she's in her own little world again and not paying any attention to us. In that respect it won't be so different, though I worry about the dangers."

"I s'pect she's just excited about her trip."

We told Scarlett she could go to Saint Jo with our witchy friend, Rose Stout, who lived with us all last year and most of the past winter before headin' to Texas Hill Country to stock up on roots, herbs, scorpion milk, and whatever else she needs for doctorin' Kansas folk. She sent word she's comin' through Dodge tomorrow and wanted to repay our hospitality by givin' me and Gentry two weeks to ourselves.

I reckon I spent a long time thinkin' these thoughts, 'cause Gentry's lookin' at me, expectin' conversation. I ain't unskilled at dinner talk, it's just that years of trail ridin' hardened me against it, 'cause most of the time it was just me and my old horse, Major, or me and my best friend, Shrug, who talks less than Major. It ain't a friendly habit I've learnt, but a practical one, since a man who talks at night in Indian country's apt to find himself buried to his neck in a red ant hill by dawn. Here at home it's different, a' course. Gentry expects conversation, and I'm glad to oblige, when reminded, or prodded. So I think a minute and start things off by sayin', "Sam's Hill."

"What?"

"A while ago you asked, 'What in Sam Hill's wrong with you?'"

She laughs. "*That's* what's on your mind? Sam's Hill?"

I nod.

"It's an expression, Emmett."

"I know," I say. "I heard it all my life."

"So what's the problem?"

"I was just wonderin' how it came to be an expression. I mean, was Sam Hill a man's name? Or was his name Sam somethin' else, and he happened to have a hill on his property?"

She looks at me like I claimed to know the colors of the moon glow. Then says, "Does it really matter? It's an expression. Who *cares* how it came to be?"

I give her a look.

She puts her hand on mine and says, "I'm sorry, Emmett. I shouldn't have over-spoke your effort at conversation. I wasn't expecting it is all." She takes a deep breath and says, "I'll bet it was the second thing you said: that a man named Sam had a gigantic hill. And this hill was so big that everyone who ever saw it told everyone they met about it, and word spread. Then people kept saying it to each other, even though they never saw the hill themselves."

"You think somethin' strange was happenin' on Sam's Hill? Somethin' people couldn't comprehend?"

She shows me a curious look. "You mean like the way people can't comprehend how Scarlett and Rose talk to snakes and see things before they happen?"

"Could be somethin' like that."

Gentry says, "Why would you think that about Sam's Hill?"

"'Cause of the way people say the expression. Like what in Sam's Hill's goin' *on*? Or like, "What in the Sam Hill are you gonna do with that gun?"

Gentry nods. "That's a clever observation, Emmett."

"You think?"

She nods.

We're both quiet till I say, "I've got another one. You know how people say Scarlett makes 'em feel better just by standin' near her?"

"That's witchery talk."

"Maybe so, but it's true. We ain't been sick a day since she turned three, and the Philadelphia folk are convinced she throws off healin' qualities like fire throws off heat."

"What's your point?"

"I can only think of one person who ain't happier for bein' around Scarlett: the new school marm. Why do you think that is?"

Gentry cocks her head. "I don't know. But again, you've surprised me. That's an excellent observation."

We concentrate on our dinner a few minutes. Then I say, "That must've been some kind of hill Sam had, for people to still be talkin' about it after all these years."

"I'll bet it was in the Texas Hill Country," Gentry says. "You think Rose has seen it?"

"If it's there I guarantee she has. But I don't reckon Sam's Hill is in Texas. I been all through that part of the country myself, and reckon I've seen every hill they got."

I notice Gentry beamin' at me, and ask what brought such a sweet smile to her face.

"I like talking to you."

"You do? How come?"

"You always find a way to surprise me. Even when I think you've got nothing to say, you surprise me."

The fact that I rarely understand what causes Gentry to give me these type a' love smiles don't change the fact I know a good opportunity when I see one. Like right now, even as she's takin' a bite of biscuit. "You know what this quiet house reminds me of?" I say.

"Tell me."

"Our honeymoon night."

She laughs. "I don't recall that at all!"

"You don't?"

"Not the quiet part! As I recall we were both pretty vocal."

I grin. "Before we were half-finished, people were yellin' and dogs were barkin'."

"Dogs *were* barking," she says, smilin' at the memory.

"I bet we could give the neighbors somethin' to talk and bark about tonight," I say.

She gives me a wink. "You think?"

"I do."

She looks at Scarlett. "We should probably save that business for tomorrow night."

CHAPTER 4

AFTER DINNER I walk the short distance to the hotel to see if I can find this new dentist Gentry's so excited about. But when I see Cal Pike's clerkin', I prepare myself for frustration, since he ain't widely known for his spirited conversation.

"How's business?" I say.

"Up and down."

"And Doris?"

"So-so."

Cal's wife, Doris, is locally famous for three things: ownin' a full set of wooden teeth; smokin' ragweed cigars; and lovin' Cal, which no one else could do. It's them first two that cause trouble from time to time, since Doris has been known to smoke her stogies too short, which sets her teeth on fire, terrifies her livestock, and sends them stampedin' through the streets of Dodge.

"Does Doris still smoke them ragweed stogies?" I ask.

"Off and on."

"I ain't seen her lately."

"She's in and out."

Cal was mule-kicked in the head such that he rarely speaks more than four words at a time, few of which are weighed down by commitment.

I ask, "Has the new dentist checked in?"

"Maybe, maybe not."

I frown. "Either he has or hasn't."

He nods up and down, then shakes his head side to side.

I say, "Which is it?"

"One or the other."

"Maybe you should check your books," I say.

He bends his head over the ledger and studies it like there might be so many guests in the hotel it could take him hours to determine if one's a dentist. Truth is the hotel ain't got but twelve rooms, nine of which are booked with Philadelphians waitin' on houses to be built. I keep expectin' Cal to look up at me over his spectacles, but he won't, so I say, "I'll assume he's stayin' here, 'cause there ain't but a couple other places he could be, and neither of 'em have beds. But I won't ask you that same question again, since it appears too burdensome a chore to get a straight answer. So I'll just ask if you've seen the man at all."

"Yes and no."

"When?"

"Now and then."

"What's that mean?"

"He's in and out."

"Assumin' he's out at the present moment, you got any idea when he might be back?"

"Sooner or later."

"Did you happen to ask where he's from?"

"Once or twice."

"What'd he say?"

"Here and there."

I walk away every bit as flustered as I expected to be, though I'm thinkin' Cal Pike can probably be trusted with a secret better than any man in town.

As I head to the door I notice Peggy Pardon sweepin' her way up the hallway toward the lobby. Peggy helps clean and cook at the hotel a couple nights a week, now that her kids are old enough to be home alone. She sees me and smiles. "I bet you're lookin' for John Boone."

"I am for a fact."

"Everyone's hopin' he'll stay."

"You know much about him?"

"Just that he was enjoyin' the company of multiple women at the Winchester a short while ago, accordin' to the gossip."

"Think he's still there?"

"I do. From what I hear, it don't take him long to re-load, if you catch my meanin'." She laughs. "You won't believe what he asked me to do."

I ain't positive I want to hear what a whorin' man might ask a hotel sweepin' gal and part-time cook to do, but she tells me anway: "Mr. Boone asked me to prepare a hot bath for him."

I chuckle. "What'd you say?"

"I told him I ain't got the time, nor the resources. I said, 'Try Saint Jo!'"

"What'd he say?"

"He said Saint Jo's further east than Denver is west."

"He probably don't know there's a dozen Saint Jo's, and two in Kansas alone. But I reckon he's talkin' about the big one in Missouri."

"You think he'll settle here?"

"I have no idea." I turn to leave, then stop and ask, "You ever had a dentist work on your teeth?"

"Nope. You?"

"Nope."

"*Would* you?" I ask.

"If I was hurting badly enough I might. If it didn't cost too much."

I nod, and head for Harry Winchester's Saloon, which happens to be our biggest competitor. If you're lookin' for sportin' gals who'll service a man so fast they don't even need a bed, the Winchester's your place. That bunch of women can fast-fuck a man in the hallway, while standin' up, faster than our girls can climb the stairs! And where we charge six dollars, the Winchester girls'll take a buck and offer change. With these type a' prices, it didn't take 'em long to capture most of our local trade.

Harry's place is two blocks from the hotel. If you want to walk with me a minute I'll tell you how Reverend Murphy's family got killed by their dinner table in Springfield last July. It started when a gambler named Davis Tutt got shot in the market square by a guy calls himself

Wild Bill Hickok. While checkin' to see if Tutt was dead, the Reverend's father got a considerable amount of blood and guts on his clothes. He came home, removed his dirty duds, set 'em on the table for his wife to clean after dinner. Though she moved the clothes and wiped the table, it weren't enough to kill whatever germs got into the chicken she was cuttin' up on the same table to fry. I'm sure the whole family enjoyed their last meal, 'cause who don't like fried chicken?

But within' three days they shit themselves to death.

Wild Bill said the shootin' had to do with a gamblin' debt. Reverend Murphy says that's generally true, but says there was bad blood between 'em, 'cause accordin' to others, Hickok fathered an illegitimate child with Tutt's sister, and Tutt had been noticed payin' too much attention to Hickok's girlfriend, Susanna Moore.

I'd tell you the rest, but it ain't that interestin', and anyway, we're here. Yep, that there's the Winchester.

I push the door open and immediately see the dentist talkin' up a group of local men at a card table. It don't escape my notice he's drunk as an orchard boar, and trouble can't be far behind. As I move toward him I'm approached by two saloon whores I never seen before.

"Is it *true*, sheriff?" one of 'em says.

"Is what true?"

"We're gonna have a beauty contest and you're gonna judge?"

By the time I say, "Oh, *hell* no!" they're already out the door, spreadin' the tale. I make a move to follow 'em to put an end to this nonsense, but get sidetracked by the sound of a gunshot, and the unmistakable sound of a man's body hittin' the floor.

CHAPTER 5

I DIDN'T SEE the actual shot, but I *do* see the dentist holdin' a smokin', one-shot derringer, standin' over Eli Shed, who's oozin' blood from his chest. I draw my gun and fire a hole in the ceilin' to keep the men at the card table from shootin' the dentist. My shot causes everyone to hit the floor except for Harry Winchester, who hollers, "How stupid *are* you, Emmett? I've got bedrooms upstairs. You better hope you didn't kill someone."

I *do* hope I didn't. But then I think about it and say, "I thought your whores didn't *use* bedrooms."

He juts his jaw and says, "You'll pay to have that ceilin' repaired."

I start to say somethin' a lot more confrontational than what I wind up sayin', which is "Send me a bill." Then I look at the man who done the shootin' and ask, "Are you John Boone?"

He turns to me and says, "When they remove the bullet from this man's chest, I want it back."

"Why?"

"It was a loan, not a gift."

I give him a look to let him know that's about the stupidest thing I ever heard, but again, I don't say it. Gentry often tells me it ain't healthy to hold things in, and says I should always tell people how their words or actions make me feel inside. I'm a slow learner in that regard, 'cause I've always acted on the assumption that shootin' a man's the quickest way to let him know how I feel about what he said or done. I walk over to Eli, drop to one knee and ask, "How you feel?"

"I hate to be the cause of interrupting your business, Sheriff."

"It's no bother. You've always been the most polite card player I ever met."

"Thank you. How's Miss Gentry?"

"It's Missus. We're married now."

"You don't say!"

"We got married in Philadelphia, same day President Lincoln got shot."

"President *Lincoln* got shot?"

"You didn't know?"

"Uh uh. Did you shoot him?"

"Naw. Some other guy did. How do you feel?"

"Well, I hate to complain."

"You've got a right to."

He shows me a brave smile. "I've been better, most days."

"Why'd this dentist fella shoot you?"

"I'm not sure. He said my wife was ugly, and I told him looks aren't everything. Then he shot me."

The dentist says, "Looks *are* everything."

Eli says, "I'm not sure he's got the right temperament for dentistry."

"You may be right," I say.

"Have you seen Rose tonight? Reason I ask, if she's not too busy I'd be obliged if she'd consider checking on me, at some point."

"She's on her way from Texas, though I ain't expectin' her till tomorrow."

"You think she'll have time to see me tomorrow?"

"She was plannin' to pick my daughter up after school, and take her to Saint Jo."

"Well then, please don't bother her on my account. I don't want to be the cause of delaying their trip."

"I reckon you'll die if she don't see you," I say.

"I think I might."

"If you survive the night, I'll have her look in on you. Where will you be?"

"I haven't given it much thought."

"We can get a couple of fellas to haul you home."

"Naw, that's too much trouble. Not to mention my wife would have a fit."

"Why's that?"

"She won't want all this blood on her floor."

"We've got to take you someplace."

"That's true. Harry won't want me lying here all night."

Harry says, "That's true. Shootin's are bad for business."

"Maybe a couple of these fellas could drag me out back," Eli says.

"Works for *me*," Harry says.

I ask, "What about the wild dogs?"

"Don't you worry," Eli says. "If they get a hold of me there'll be less of me to bury, which is always an issue with this hard Kansas ground. But it's not right to put this burden on you. If someone'll be kind enough to drag me out the door I'll ask for nothing more. You've been most kind to me, and I feel terrible for taking up this much of your time."

I ask Harry if I can use his buckboard. He says he'll rent it to me. I offer him two dollars and he says it'll cost me four. I tell him I ain't got four dollars on me, and he says he'll collect it when he brings me the bill for the hole in his ceiling. "Or I can forgive the debt altogether if one of my whores wins the beauty contest."

Harry's whores couldn't win a beauty contest if the opposition was mules in a mud hole, but it don't matter, 'cause like I tell Harry: "There ain't gonna *be* no beauty contest."

"Fine. In that case, the buckboard'll cost you four bucks."

"Fine. Hitch the horses."

"Horses are two dollars more."

"Fine. But I'll want the buckboard all night."

"All night is gonna be—"

—I draw my gun. "All night is gonna be what?"

"Fine with me," he says.

I holster my gun and tell the other card players to carry Eli to the buckboard, and drive him to my place.

Eli says, "Miss—I mean Mrs. Gentry—won't want all this blood in *her* house, neither. And I can't have you spendin' six hard-earned dollars on my account."

"Don't worry about the money or the house."

"What's your plan?"

"You'll be stayin' in the buckboard, and I'll watch over you, to keep the dogs and other varmints away."

"I can't ask you to do that."

"You don't have to. I'm glad to do it."

"Well, that's more than kind. Maybe I'll bleed out quickly, and you won't have to miss much sleep."

"You might, but if you're alive and in my front yard when Rose gets to town, she won't have to waste time lookin' for you."

"I'll pay you back the six dollars here, or in the afterlife."

"It ain't an issue for me, but if it is for you, then either will be fine."

I don't tell Eli my plan, 'cause I don't want to put ideas in people's heads. But I intend to have Scarlett stand next to him tonight for a while, 'cause if she really *does* have healin' powers, I'd like Eli to benefit from 'em.

"What about the dentist?" someone asks.

"I'll take him to my office while Harry hitches the buckboard."

The whole saloon suddenly goes quiet as mice at a funeral. Someone asks, "You gonna lock him up in one of your jail cells?"

"I am."

This is a big event, since I ain't jailed a single soul in the whole year I've owned a proper jail.

Someone says, "Can we come watch?"

"No. I'm gonna lock him up, then head home. In the meantime, someone get Eli some blankets to help him weather the night. Then bring him to my place and I'll tend to him as best I can."

John Boone, the dentist, says, "What's all this about jail cells?"

I give him a look. "You can't shoot a man for agreein' his own wife is ugly."

"Where I come from you can shoot a man for anything."

"And where is it you come from, exactly?"

"Here and there."

"Well, that ain't true already. Least not the 'here' part."

"I've never spent the night in a jail cell," Boone says, "but it sounds uncomfortable."

"It'll sound even worse the second night."

"Surely you're not planning to *keep* me there."

"You'll be there till the trial, at least."

"When will *that* be?"

"Whenever the circuit judge shows up."

"When are you expecting him?"

"I ain't."

"What do you mean?"

"He don't make regular rounds to Dodge. I'll have to send a report to Wichita and wait to hear back. Since Wichita's a pretty far distance, he might not come at all, if you're the only prisoner awaitin' trial. They'll likely arrange a trial date in Wichita, or some other city, and I'll have to haul your ass there."

"That's unacceptable."

"So is killin' a man."

"This man is not dead yet."

"He's got a point, Sheriff," Eli says.

Boone says, "This town needs a dentist in the worst way, but there's not much good I can do sitting in a jail cell for weeks or months. On the other hand, if you can see fit to forgive this little misunderstanding...."

"That ain't gonna happen. How did you come to call his wife ugly in the first place?" I ask.

"We were discussing the beauty contest."

"I figured as much. I'm guessin' this stupid contest was your idea."

"This contest, far from being stupid, is designed to unite the community, by not only respecting, but celebrating, the singular beauty of Dodge City women, and those from the surrounding counties. When we, as a town, advertise that this pocket of Kansas has the prettiest women west of the Mississippi, settlers will flock here in droves."

"I s'pect this contest was designed to drum up business, so you could charge girls and women for fixin' their smiles."

"I won't deny the marketing component."

"The what?"

"In larger cities, drumming up business is called marketing."

"In smaller towns it's called troublemakin'. You ain't been here 24 hours and the whole town's about to unravel. Now let's get goin!"

CHAPTER 6

AFTER FORMALLY ARRESTIN' John Boone and lockin' him up, I swing by the hotel and have Peggy Pardon gather and inventory his belongin's, then watch as Cal Pike locks 'em in the hotel's coat closet. Then I make him cancel Boone's room so he won't be charged for it. Then I go home and wait for the buckboard. When it arrives, we tie the horses to one of my hitchin' posts, and the card players who drove it give Eli a bottle of rye, offer their well-wishes, and tell him they'll check on him tomorrow.

Eli says, "Fellas, I can't drink all this whiskey by myself. I'd welcome you to stay and drink with me a bit."

One says, "We would, but Mr. Winchester said he'd only hold our places at the table for thirty minutes, and we've already used half that."

"Well, you better get going, then. Good luck to you."

When the men leave, I say, "I'll have a taste with you."

"Thanks, Sheriff."

I enjoy a couple swallows with him, then go inside to tell Gentry what happened, and ask if I can bring Scarlett outside for a few minutes. At first Gentry don't want Scarlett exposed to a bloody gunshot victim, but when I tell her Scarlett's presence might help him feel better, she says, "Light a lamp, Emmett, and we'll both come out."

Moments later we're all standing around the buckboard. "Eli, you remember Gentry. And you probably can't see her from inside the buckboard, but our daughter's here, too: Scarlett."

Eli says, "Well, hey there, Mrs. Gentry. Congratulations on marrying Emmett. You got yourself a good man right here."

"Thank you, Eli."

"My pleasure. And Scarlett, if you're half as pretty as your ma—" he suddenly cries out in pain, then apologizes for startling her, and adds, "I'm sure you'll win that beauty contest. Unless your ma enters it."

Gentry says, "What beauty contest?"

He don't answer, so she looks at me.

I shrug like I don't know.

Gentry turns back to Eli and says, "What's happened? Who shot you?"

"Emmett didn't say?"

"No. And I wonder why."

"Well, I hate to spread gossip."

"I don't think this qualifies as gossip, Eli."

"Still, I don't want to make you feel less about the man, especially since I know you hold him in high esteem."

34

He gasps from the pain and apologizes a second time.

Gentry turns to me.

I say, "It was John Boone, the dentist."

"That's impossible," she says.

"I was right there when it happened."

"I was, too," Eli says.

Gentry says, "What on earth did you do to provoke such a response from a man who eases the pain and suffering of women and children?"

"I take full responsibility," Eli says. Then adds, "Sheriff, I'm not going to press charges. Dodge needs a dentist, and Dr. Boone's right about not bein' able to provide treatment from a jail cell."

"That's thoughtful of you, but it ain't up to you to press or not press charges. The man shot you plain as day, and he'll stand trial for it."

"I'm sure it was self-defense," Gentry says. "Did you come at him with a gun or knife?"

"Well, I was unarmed," Eli says, "and sittin' down at the time he shot me, but givin' him the benefit of the doubt, I can see where he might have thought I'd be a threat, after what he said."

I look at Scarlett in the lamplight. Barefoot, in her nightgown, she looks tiny; thin as a reed, and fragile. I notice she's standin' stock-still, starin' straight ahead, like she's concentratin' real hard. I say, "You feel any better, Eli?"

"I'm not one to advertise my problems, but since you brought it up, this last couple of minutes has been the worst pain of my life. I fear I'm a goner, Sheriff."

I frown.

Scarlett sees me lookin' at her, spins around, walks back in the house.

"Be right back," I say, followin' close behind.

She walks straight to her room, sits on her bed, folds her arms.

I sit beside her and say, "A lot of people believe you have healin' abilities."

"I know."

"If you do, there's a man outside can sure use some."

"I know."

"Is there anythin' you can do to help him?"

She says nothin'.

"Scarlett?"

She takes her time, but finally says, "It doesn't matter. He'll be dead in ten minutes."

"You're sure?"

"Yes sir."

"Is there *nothin'* you can do?"

"I *won't* help him."

"*Excuse* me?"

"I *could* help him...but I won't."

"Why not?"

"He's a bad man."

"*That* can't be true. Why, you heard the way he talks. I reckon he's the most polite man I ever met!"

"He killed a woman."

"*What?*"

"Killed her and stole her money."

"When?"

"This morning, while I was getting slapped."

"Dodge is a very small town, Scarlett. I reckon I'd a' heard if some woman got killed this mornin'."

"You'll hear it soon enough."

"Who do you think he killed?"

"His wife."

I take a minute to wonder if that could possibly be true, then hear Eli groanin' outside and decide it don't matter. I ask, "Honey, how does this healin' thing work?"

"It just does."

"Is it somethin' you can turn on and off?"

"No sir. If I do nothing, people feel better. They heal from inside out."

"Eli didn't."

She smiles. "I was hurting him worse."

"Because you thought he killed his wife?"

"Yes sir."

I sigh. "Even if he did, it don't make you a better person to let a man suffer if he don't have to."

"I don't *want* to be a better person...at least, not to *him*!"

"Why not?"

"He looks at me funny."

"What do you mean?"

"In the school yard."

"When?"

"Every day."

"What do you mean?"

"He gives me candy and asks me to show him my underpants, and what's inside them."

"He—*What*? Wait. You're talkin' about...your *under drawers*?"

"Yes sir."

"You ever show him?"

"No sir."

"Good girl."

I stomp outside, grab Eli by the hair, lift him two feet in the air, and punch him square in the face. Then I throw him back onto the floor of the buckboard so fast he ain't had time to scream yet.

But Gentry has: "*Emmett! For the love of God!* What are you *doing? What's gotten into you?"

"I don't want to talk about it," I say, stormin' back into the house even as she's rushin' to tend to Eli. By now he's yellin' somethin' awful, and I'm shakin' with rage. I pick up a chair and throw it against the wall. Then take a deep breath and say, "Scarlett, I understand why you wanted to hurt that man. I done somethin' to hurt him, too, just now. It weren't right, and I'll probably get a black mark against my name for that act of cruelty, but I'll admit to feelin' better for hurtin' him with my own hand before turnin' him over to God."

"What's God going to do with him?"

"I s'pect He'll judge them things Eli done wrong, and decide what to do with his eternal soul. But in the meantime, if there's somethin' you can do to ease his pain, or make him feel better, I'd like you to do it."

"Why?"

"Because it's the Christian thing to do."

"I *won't!*"

"You *will*, and you'll do it *now!*"

She tosses her hair. "Maybe I'll show him my underpants."

I grit my teeth and say, "*Ease his pain, Scarlett!*"

She juts her chin at me and scrunches her little face into an angry scowl. "I won't do it!"

"*Now*, Scarlett!"

Her face turns three shades of purple like her ma.

I say, "I won't ask you again."

She slants her eyes into slits of anger, says, "*Fine!*" Then screams and I hear what sounds like a cannon shot outside our front door. Gentry shrieks and comes runnin' into the house.

"What the *hell?*" I say.

"*Eli!*" she shouts. "Oh, my *God!* Oh, my *God! Eli!*"

"What about him?"

"His—his head just burst into flames!"

I turn to deal with Scarlett, but she's already closed her bedroom door. For a split second I can't decide whether to spank Scarlett or comfort Gentry, but then I see beams of light flashin' furiously under Scarlett's door, and decide it ain't in our best interest to provoke a child who can start face fires by yellin'. I reach out to Gentry, who shakes and sobs in my arms a full minute before sayin', "What happened, Emmett?"

I can't think of nothin' to say, except, "She's got your temper."

"Who?"

"Our daughter."

She draws back. "Why would you *say* such a thing?"

I point to the front window. I can't see the buckboard from this angle, but I see the flames. Which reminds me....

"Shit! The buckboard!"

She gives me a look, cause it's a well-known fact we're not supposed to say shit in the house, but I run past her and out the door and pull Eli's flamin' body from the buckboard, then take my shirt off and start floggin' the buckboard flames. Gentry's right behind me, runnin' a pail to the well. Within minutes we've got the fire out, though the buckboard ain't much to look at.

Gentry wipes a thick hank of hair from her face and parks it behind her ear, leavin' a black smudge on her face. She looks at Eli's body and says, "For a man who hated to be a burden all his life, he sure caused a lot of grief tonight." She sighs, looks at me. "Why did you hit that poor man, and what did you mean about Scarlett's temper?"

"I blew his head up," Scarlett says, from behind us.

"This isn't a time for tall tales, young lady," Gentry scolds.

"It ain't a tall tale," I say.

"I got mad," Scarlett says.

Gentry gives me a look. "I'm supposed to believe her temper caused Eli's head to burst into flames?"

"You got a better explanation?"

She looks at Scarlett. "What do you mean you got mad?"

Scarlett shrugs.

I ask, "What were all them colors comin' from under your door?"

"I was fighting to hold my temper."

Gentry's lookin' half-furious, half-confused, half-exhausted. That's probably too many halves, but the bottom line is she's about to get a mood. Before she has a chance to, I tell her, "Stay here a minute. I'll be right back."

I walk Scarlett back inside, tuck her into bed and say, "That was a scary thing you done just now."

"I know."

"And you talked back to me. Multiple times."

"I was mad."

"I know it's hard to keep your emotions steady when you're upset, but you can't just go around blowin' people's heads up."

"I know."

"Look at me."

She does.

"What you did to Eli worries me. If you can't hold your temper any better than that, I have to wonder who might be next."

"What do you mean?"

"If you ever get mad at your ma, so mad you start to think bad thoughts, you'd best send 'em my way."

"Why?"

"'Cause that lady's the love of my life. If someone harms a hair on her head they'll get a bullet 'tween their eyes in short order."

"You'd shoot your own daughter?"

"I ain't sayin' it'd give me pleasure."

"That's a vile thing to say."

"I'm only sayin' what needs to be said."

"I would never hurt you or Mama."

"No matter how angry you got?"

"I would never hurt you or Mama."

"How can you be so sure?"

"Rose put a thought about it in my head."

"Is that what them colors was all about?"

She nods.

I say, "How strong is that thought in your head?"

"Real strong."

"How long is it likely to last?"

"Till the day I die, plus a week."

I can't think why she'd need an extra week after she dies, but it brings me enough comfort to say, "I'm sorry I threatened to put a bullet between your eyes. I could never do that."

"Did Rose put a thought in your head about it?"

"Nope. Your ma put that thought in my head the day you were born."

She looks at me in a funny way, like she just had a thought and can't decide whether to tell it, but finally says, "Mama's gun can't shoot you."

"What do you mean?"

"I spoke words over it."

I ain't sure what that means, nor why she said it, but it puts me in mind that last year Rose claimed she spoke words over me and Bose Rennick, the outlaw, such that neither of us could shoot the other as long as we're in Kansas.

Not that we ain't tried! In fact, we pot-shotted each other numerous times, but our guns only clicked and our bullets wouldn't fire. Rose never said why she done that, nor how long it would last, but if you happen to hear two guns clickin' away in Kansas, you'll know it's me and Bose, testin' our weapons on each other.

I give Scarlett a hug. "I love you, honey."

"Thank you, Papa."

After kissin' her goodnight, I head outside to where Gentry's waitin', take a deep breath, and tell her how Scarlett came to blow up Eli's head.

When I finish, Gentry says, "Her *under* garments?"

I nod.

She walks over to Eli's smolderin' body, hikes her nightgown up to her hips, squats, and pisses on his corpse. As I walk over to comfort her the buckboard crashes and a heavy piece of it lands on my foot.

"*Shit!*" I say, not carin' if Gentry scolds me or not. And anyway, I weren't *in* the house when I said it. I fall to the ground in agony, and roll around.

Gentry rushes to my side. "How bad is it?"

"The buckboard?"

"Your foot."

"It hurts. I s'pect I'll be limpin' for at least six chapters."

CHAPTER 7

THE FIRST PIE shows up in my office at 9:30 a.m., courtesy of May Gray.

"What's this?" I ask.

"I know how you love my rhubarb pie," May says.

"I do for a fact. But what's the occasion? It ain't my birthday."

"I was just thinking about you, and that time you came over to my house for dinner. Do you remember?"

"It's somethin' I'll never forget. And even if I could, I doubt Gentry would let me."

Her face flushes.

Mine does too.

May Gray's the widow who cut my hair, shaved my beard, and pulled my pecker two years ago.

She says, "I wanted to ask you about the beauty contest."

I frown. "There ain't no beauty contest, May."

She laughs. "Of *course* there is. The whole *town's* talking about it."

"Old Dodge has already got wind of this?"

"Of course."

May and about thirty people still live twelve miles away, in Old Dodge. They're happy with their homes and won't move to the new location till we finish buildin' all the common buildin's a town ought to have, like a church, a school, and a town hall. We got the school and half the church, but town meetin's are still generally held at the *Lucky Spur*.

She glances at the door that leads to the jail cells. "Have you released Mr. Boone yet?"

"Nope."

She lowers her voice. "But you're *going* to, right? Everyone says it was self-defense."

"It weren't."

"But—"

"I was there."

"But Eli killed Mable, didn't he?"

"It appears so. I found her dead in their bed."

"I heard there was a note?"

"It were just three words, written on the sheet in her own blood: 'Eli did this.' I reckon she wrote that just before passin'."

"If Mr. Boone killed Eli, he's done nothing worse than kill a murderer."

"That's true."

"So you'll let him go?"

"Nope."

"Why not?"

"He has to stand trial, for murder."

"If Eli had lived, *he'd* have stood trial for murdering Mable."

"That's right. And he would've been found guilty."

"And what would his punishment have been?"

"Death by hangin'."

"In essence, Mr. Boone is a hero."

"I don't know what essence is, but I wouldn't call the man a hero in any case."

"Well, you can't deny he saved the community the time and expense of a trial."

"Maybe so, but that don't make him innocent of murder."

"Well, I expect this is all new to you, Emmett. There are two bodies to bury, and a town to heal. I'm sure you'll see things differently in a few days."

"I doubt it."

She pauses a moment, then says, "Is Gentry planning to enter the contest?"

"No, she is not."

May breathes a sigh of relief. Then says, "You know my daughter, Ellie."

"I do indeed, though I ain't seen her in a while."

"She's twelve now, so I keep a tight rein on her, as you can imagine."

"You're smart to do that," I say, fully aware that twelve's the age of consent. While it's true that girls can marry at ten with their parent's permission, twelve-year-old girls can do what they want, legally.

"Which of us should enter?" May says, "Ellie or me?"

"Neither. 'Cause there ain't gonna be no beauty contest."

"I don't know why you keep saying that. Everyone in town's making plans."

I take a deep breath, hold my tongue.

May smiles, pats my hand. "I suppose if there ever *is* a beauty contest, Ellie and I could *both* enter."

I reckon she's right, but in a contest between the two, Ellie would almost certainly prevail. I ain't seen her more'n a couple of times since she was ten, but I've seen May numerous times, includin' naked two years ago, and "beauty" ain't the word that come to my mind that day, nor since.

She asks if she can visit with John Boone for a few minutes, and I let her do so, then bid her goodbye. When she leaves, Boone says, "Sheriff, I understand you and your wife own all the commercial land in New Dodge."

"We did at one time, but we've been sellin' and tradin' pieces away for different stores and businesses."

"But you still have numerous lots available."

"We do."

"I'd like to purchase one on Main Street."

"Why?"

"To open a business, of course."

"I were you, I'd wait till after your trial."

"Perhaps I should take the matter up with your wife." He closes his eyes, lifts his head, and sniffs like a bull, tryin' to scent a cow. "Ah, Gentry!" he says, and sniffs again. "How many men has she sent home with smiles on their faces?"

"She ain't in the business."

"Of course she is! She hooked me up with three different women yesterday."

"She don't service customers."

"Of course she does! She personally made sure my whiskey was regularly replenished."

"What I'm sayin', she don't do any whorin'."

"Ah! But she used to."

"Who told you that?"

"I didn't *need* to be told. It's the most obvious thing in town. Sheriff, I've been around whores my whole life. Working ones, like your Mary Burns; reformed ones, like...well, I shouldn't say; and former ones, like your wife, Gentry. And the one thing they all have in common is the way they size a man up when meeting him the first time."

"That's bullshit."

"If it were bullshit, you'd be denying it. Watch her face next time she's introduced to a man. No, don't *watch* her face, *study* it. I guarantee you'll see a different look. It'll only take her an instant, but in that instant she'll check him out. By that I mean she'll try to imagine four things: first, what's his net worth? Second, what type of man is he? In other words, is he likely to woo or hurt her? Is he the type who might fall in love if she works him properly? Can she string him along and turn him into a long-term customer? Third, she'll try to picture him naked, which isn't as titillating as it sounds. What I mean is, she'll play guessing games with herself over what's to be found under his clothes. Scars, bruises, cuts, sores, filth, stink...whatever. Fourth, she'll picture what life with him would be like if they were together. And Sheriff, the most amazing thing about whores, whether current or otherwise, they make all these mental calculations in the space of seconds. It's fascinating! Don't take my word for it, study her face next chance you get. You'll see I'm right."

By noon there are four pies and three batches of cookies on my desk, which ain't no small achievement considerin' there's only eight stoves in the whole town and two of 'em are mine! Each girl or woman who brought these delights said the same thing: "I don't want you to think I'm bribin' you, but—"

And then they mentioned the beauty contest and asked such questions as: "Is it just looks or will we be judged on talent as well?" Or, "Which type of girl is likely to fare better: sturdy or frail?" Or, "How important is complexion (or wardrobe, or teeth?)" The "teeth" part threw me at first, 'cause I wondered how a woman with no teeth might hope to win a beauty contest. But then I realized they're askin' if a woman with yellow, black, or brown teeth might be at a disadvantage, and the answer would have been *yes*, had I been disposed to *give* an answer, which I weren't.

Of course, they all wanted to know if Gentry was plannin' to enter, or if Rose might, since them two are widely regarded the prettiest women ever to step foot in Kansas. After them, you'd have a wide gap before and after Penelope Way, her bein' part of the original six who moved here from Philadelphia nine months ago. A' course, we didn't have to journey outside of Kansas to bring beauty to Dodge. Our own Lillie Gee was every bit as pretty as Penelope, but unfortunately, she caught a bullet and became the only resident of

Dodge ever buried indoors. We laid her to rest under the kitchen floor at the *Spur*.

After Penelope, a judge would probably pick the astonishin'ly ample-chested Enorma Suiters, and she'd be followed by Dodge's only ten-dollar whore, Tootie Green, who always tells this same joke to new customers:

"I don't wear underwear," she says, "And one day, while descending a buckboard, I had to climb over a drunk who was lying face-up in the street. Moments later a fella asked the drunk, 'Was that Tootie Green?' and he said, 'Naw, it was brown and furry, just as you'd expect!'"

Now that I think on it, Tootie's good at what John Boone calls marketin', since all them customers go around the country repeatin' her joke to whoever they meet, and she's become famous, since everyone wants to see her tootie for themselves!

After Tootie Green, well...that's about as far as you can stretch the beauty part of any contest.

That ain't to say the womenfolk of Dodge are a homely bunch.

They are, but that ain't what I was sayin'.

To be fair, all the Philadelphia women are generally presentable, and two of 'em are quite well-formed, though I keep that opinion completely to myself. Havin' said that, it's no secret the well-formed ones suffer from faces so severe they'd scare the hump off a Brahma bull.

There are some cute young'uns in our town, of course, and it strikes me if I ever had to judge a beauty contest, the easy way out would be to pick a cute child. A 'course, the womenfolk wouldn't go for it, nor does it matter, since I have no intention of judgin' a beauty contest in the first place.

However many women, girls, and children are in Old and New Dodge, there ain't but one can be called the ugliest without gettin' an argument: Shrug's sad old girlfriend, Ella Foreskin. Ella's so shortchanged of looks and personality her name can't be spoken without shudderin'. If a man knows she's headin' toward town he'll stop what he's doin' and sound an alarm so his friends and loved ones can warn their eyes. I'm not sayin' this about Ella to be mean, but 'cause I'm standin' by my window, watchin' her boyfriend scamper crab-like toward my office with a bottle of whiskey around his neck. I open the door for him and say, "Not you, too!"

Shrug laughs and signs that there ain't enough whiskey in Kansas to put Ella in a beauty contest. I smile as he signs Rudy would have a better chance of winnin', and he's a bear. He indicates Ella has qualities he prizes above her looks, which pleases me to hear, since in all the time I've known Ella I can't think of *any* qualities she might have that Shrug might prize. Before I think too hard on it, Shrug makes a rude gesture to show exactly what he prizes about Ella, though thoughts of doin' that with her don't carry my thoughts to the lofty heights he's describin'.

He sees the look on my face and laughs.

I say, "If the whiskey ain't a bribe for Ella to win the beauty contest, why'd you bring it?"

He signs it's for drinkin' with cookies and pie, and for makin' my foot feel less sore. I nod, thinkin', *all them town women came to my office today, but the only person thoughtful enough to ask about my foot was Shrug.*

I say, "Thanks for bringin' whiskey instead of Rag Soup."

He gestures the Rag Soup would heal me in a day, but I tell him I'd suffer worse by drinkin' it. He makes a rude gesture at me for makin' the comment. I return the gesture, and we laugh and take a pull from his bottle. Holdin' the liquor in my mouth so I can feel the burn before swallowin', I look at Shrug, in case he wants to sign about the whiskey, but he's content to enjoy the taste in silence, and that suits me just fine.

As a young boy, Shrug's body was crushed in a stampede. He healed sideways, which turned out to be useful in some ways, such as chuckin' rocks and scamperin' lightnin'-speed across the plains. But it also left him unable to ride a horse, so he has to carry everything he travels with in slings around his body. This includes his throwin' rocks, tools, food, and medicines, which include the berries, herbs, and tree bark he gathers from place to place. He wraps these up in rags and travels great distances with 'em, which rubs the ingredients together and bleeds 'em into the fabric of the rags. When him or me or someone else needs serious doctorin', Shrug'll boil some water in the small pot he carries, and dump the rags in there till it makes a foul-ass soup that'll give you the worst case of cramps and shits you ever had.

But when that part's done, and you finally get some sleep, you tend to wake up cured.

Sometimes it takes an extra day, and it ain't a pleasant one. But after that, you'll feel better.

We take another pull, and he signs a question about last night. I ain't sure what all he's heard about the events, so I tell him everythin', includin' how the women of Dodge want me to release John Boone, 'cause they feel we need a dentist. We take another swig and I sigh and tell him how this damn beauty contest came to be and speculate on how it got out of hand so fast and how it could divide the town. We have another swig, and I sigh again and tell him if I judge the contest every man, woman, and child in the county will hate me for not pickin' their ma, sis, daughter, or granny. We have another swig, and I sigh again. Before long I find myself swiggin' without the sigh. We dig into a couple of pies, sample the cookies, and drink some more. By the time Shrug leaves, it's late afternoon, and nearly time to fetch Scarlett from school. I lean back in my chair, close my eyes, and enjoy the glow from the bourbon for twelve seconds, when the door suddenly opens and in walks Penelope Way.

She ain't carryin' cookies or pie.

But she *is* wearin' a huge smile.

CHAPTER 8

ACCORDIN' TO GENTRY, Penelope Way has been sweet on me since the day we met.

Accordin' to Gentry, out of all the women in the world, the only one she fears losin' me to is Penelope.

Accordin' to Gentry, any woman can name the woman who's the biggest threat to her marriage.

And accordin' to Gentry, that woman is Penelope Way.

Hearin' them words come out of Gentry's mouth on several occasions might be the reason I'm starin' at Penelope the way I am, 'stead of askin' why she's here.

Or maybe it's 'cause I've had more whiskey today than I usually drink in a week.

But I don't think it's the liquor.

I think it's Penelope, and what Gentry said about her.

She's starin' at me, too, not sayin' a word.

Like I said before, she ain't as pretty as Gentry or Rose, but for reasons I can't explain, Penelope's turnin' prettier by the moment as she stands there, starin' into my eyes. People say I'm fearsome good at readin' eyes and expressions, which helps when dealin' with Indians, outlaws, and quick-draw shootists, but my ability to cipher eyes and expressions don't extend to women such as Gentry and Penelope.

Especially Penelope.

The look in her eyes is sorrowful. Yearnin'. Compellin', and whatever's goin' on between us is meltin' the whole room around us and puttin' a charge in the air like the type you'd find in a damp field in the summer, after a lightin' strike. She parts her lips and flicks them lightly with her tongue, and I suddenly feel like I'm suffocating.

"Dear Emmett," she says.

"What?"

"How's your poor foot?"

"You're married."

"We sure are!" she says.

"I love Gentry."

"How could you not? She's amazing!"

"And you love Oliver."

She don't comment on that, but says, "I've always wondered what it would be like to be married to a person who's perfect in every possible way."

"You have?"

"I envy Gentry. We all do."

"Why?"

"The others envy her beauty, her sweetness, her kind, caring manner, her temperament, her grace, and humor. They're amazed by her charm."

"But not you?"

"I admire *all* those qualities Gentry has in abundance. But that's not the reason I *envy* her."

"It ain't?"

"Not at all. I'm envious of two things only."

"What's the first thing?"

Her sad smile tugs at my heart with a gentle, unsteady pain, like when Shrug or Gentry cut splinters from my foot with a huntin' knife. She says, "I'm envious Gentry has *you*, Emmett, and can cradle you in her arms, morning, noon, and night; and can kiss you nonstop, and give you all the womanly joys you deserve, anytime you're in need, no matter how tired she might be; and can live for you, and dote on your every care and concern."

"You envy *that*?"

"Who wouldn't?"

I would have thought *no* one, till she just said it. But now I'm wonderin' if it's just her, that would envy it, since Gentry don't treat me that way. I mean, she treats me fine, and I never had no complaints over the attention she offers. But these things Penelope's sayin' sound like a whole different style of treatment altogether, and compels me to ask, "What's the second thing you envy about Gentry?"

"That she's perfect."

"Huh?"

Penelope's eyes dig into mine with all the serious urgency I felt years ago when rescuin' Shrug from a collapsed cave. It almost feels like she's tryin' to rescue me from a serious problem I didn't' even know I had till she told me about it. Then she says, "I envy the fact that Gentry's perfect in every way. In *every*...way."

"Why, Gentry ain't perfect," I say.

She takes a quick step closer. "She's *not?*"

"Well, a' course not." I want to add that *no one's* perfect, but that Gentry's as close to perfect as a man could wish for—but that don't come out of my mouth, for some reason. I feel my mouth movin', like it's *tryin'* to form the words, but there's no sound to go with 'em.

"Do you find me the least bit attractive, Emmett?"

"At this very moment?"

"Yes."

"Painfully so."

"Why, *thank you* Emmett! I believe that's the nicest thing you've ever said to me."

She kisses me.

Kisses me?

Yup. In fact, she's *still* kissin' me.

I never saw it comin'.

One second she's talkin', the next, she's kissin'! I take a few seconds to wonder how this came to be, then realize I should probably end the kiss first, and work out the whys and wherefores later.

So that's what I do: back out from under the kiss.

Now she's givin' me a look that's meant for the bedroom, and I wonder how the temperature managed to rise ten degrees in the past 20 seconds. She looks like she's burstin' to say somethin', but can't quite get up the courage.

While she's tryin', I take a moment to wonder besides Penelope's uncommon beauty, what Gentry sees in her that could possibly make me leave the woman I love. The curiosity pulls on me as fiercely as May Gray pulled on my pecker that time, and the fact we're both flushed, and silent, makes the whole situation practically intoxicatin'.

Finally, she says, "Have you ever wondered what my body looks like, under all these clothes?"

"Uh..."

"I know you'd never want to *see* me without clothes, since you love Gentry so much, but I wouldn't mind if you wondered about it."

"Well..."

"Emmett?"

"Yeah?"

"I've never asked you for a favor, have I?"

"I don't believe so."

"If I were going to ask you for one right now, do you know what it would be?"

"Nope."

"I'd have you close your eyes and think about me."

"You would?"

She nods.

"You mean now?"

"No, Emmett."

"When?"

"Tonight, when Gentry's making love to you, giving herself to you, touching you in all the ways you want to be touched. If you'd do that for me, just once, you'd know how

I feel. Because I think about touching you and making love to you every single night of my life."

"You do?"

"I do. And you know what else? Every morning I day-dream what it would be like to be in your bed."

"It's just a regular bed."

"I mean, to be in your bed and wake up beside you."

From somewhere deep in my heart I muster up the strength to say, "I don't like to refuse grantin' favors, but that one about thinkin' of you in that way ain't proper."

She smiles. "Of course it isn't. Because you're married to Gentry, and I'm married to what's-his-name."

"Oliver."

"Exactly. But that's what makes it so much fun! It would be our little secret, Emmett. And before you say it's wrong to have secrets from Gentry and Oliver, I'll bet you and Wayne Newton tell each other lots of things you don't share with Gentry."

"That's true enough," I say.

The Wayne Newton she's talkin' about is Shrug, who's actual name is Wayne. Though he's a Newton, I ain't heard him called that in years. He's from Newton, Kansas, a town 20 miles north of here that was named for his grandfather, Issac, who was the first person to settle in that area. Shrug don't like to think about Newton much, since that's where he got crushed in the stampede.

"It's not like we're doing anything wrong," Penelope says. "You'd just be thinking of me, while making love to Gentry. And if she refuses her charms, you'd close your eyes and think of me anyway, and how I'd never, ever, refuse to share my charms. Emmett?"

"Huh?"

"I can't tell you how much it would please me to enter this very office tomorrow and see from the look on your face that we're both sharing this special secret instead of just me."

"*I won't do it!*" I say, surprisin' myself.

She smiles. "You won't be able *not* to, my love!"

CHAPTER 9

I'M STANDIN' IN front of the school house, waitin' on
Scarlett. Miss Gilmore sees me and comes out with an even
bigger frown than she wore yesterday. I hope to hell Scarlett
didn't tell her about makin' Eli's head burst into flames, or
that I offered to shoot her 'tween the eyes if she ever hurt
Gentry.

"Sheriff, this has to stop."

"What's happened?"

"I had to rap Scarlett's knuckles with a ruler."

"How come?"

She eyes me carefully before sayin', "I don't know what
goes on inside the walls of your home when you're not
planning beauty contests and such, so I'm compelled to ask
if you *ever* discipline this child? Because it's clear to me your
approach to raising her is slipshod at best."

"Ma'am?"

"It can't be easy raising a child who possesses the intelligence and vocabulary of a Harvard scholar. But allowing her to engage in flights of fantasy where she pretends to talk to snakes, tells fortunes, and heals the sick, is setting a very dangerous precedent."

I don't understand half of what she just said, but the part about havin' a very dangerous president gives me pause. We just lost Abe Lincoln, and Kansas folk have been extra skittish worryin' about the new fella who took over for him. While Abe weren't considered dangerous, he also weren't able to avoid the Great War, so if the new president's *particularly* dangerous, it's bad news indeed.

When Miss Gillmore sees I'm properly concerned, she goes back to talkin' about Scarlett: "Your daughter believes in witches and speaks with a vulgarity that surpasses the crudest I've experienced."

"What words did she say?"

"The sort I would never repeat, nor should *anyone*, if I had my way. To put it bluntly, her words were unfit for human ears."

"I'll have a talk with her."

"You'd better. Because if these incidents are to be routine, I'm afraid your Scarlett will find herself unwelcome in my classroom."

I motion Scarlett outside, lead her down the steps, and over to the hitchin' rail. Before I even open my mouth she says, "Miss Gilmore hates me."

"No she don't."

"She hates me and hates the truth."

"What do you mean?"

"Every time I tell the truth, she punishes me."

"That can't be right."

"It is. And, she's a *liar!*"

I put my finger to my lips so she'll hush a moment, while I look around to make sure no one's close enough to hear my daughter callin' the county's teacher a liar. Scarlett's manner of speakin' is rare for a child, and I ain't experienced in dealin' with *any* type of kids, much less them who're smarter than me. Rose says Scarlett's not just rare, but one-of-a-kind, and recommends me and Gentry give her a wide berth in the way she expresses herself, as someday she's gonna save the whole town from dyin' from a horrible disease.

"You shouldn't call people liars," I say.

"Even when they *are?*"

I remove my hat and try to think up a sentence that makes me sound smarter than I am. It takes a minute, but I finally come up with, "What's the source of this accusation?"

She gives me a funny look; then says, "Miss Gilmore says we should always tell the truth."

"Well, you should."

"And I do. But she can't *handle* the truth."

I look at my way-too-smart-for-her-age daughter. "Are you sure you're only five?"

"Almost five. You ask me that every day."

"What'd you say that got your knuckles rapped?"

She shrugs. "The smallest true thing you could ever imagine."

"Let's hear it."

"I told her I was a bastard."

"You...*what?*"

"I told her the truth: you were married when I was born, but not to Mama."

I give her a double look. Then say, "At the time you were born, I thought my first wife, Amy, had been killed by Indians."

"All the more reason you should have married Mama before procreating."

"I ain't sure what that means, young lady, but it sounds disrespectful. And I won't have disrespectful talk from a child."

"Now you sound like Jean."

"Who's Jean?"

"Miss Gilmore."

"I don't expect Miss Gilmore wants to be called Jean by her students."

"Why not? It's her name."

I take my bandana out of my back pocket, wipe my forehead, tie it around my neck, and put my hat back on.

She says, "Are you done?"

"What do you mean?"

"You usually take your hat off and rub your hair when you need time to think."

"This situation calls for deeper thought than I can coax from my hat, but I'm gonna share somethin' with you I learned a long time ago: just 'cause somethin's true don't mean it's proper to say."

"Why not?"

"If one of your friends asks how you're feelin', and you've got a rash on your rump that's oozin' pus would you tell 'em?"

"I don't have any friends."

"Say you did. Would you tell 'em your butt's on fire?"

"Yes."

I believe she would, which means I gave a bad example. If she were a wilderness child I could give her a dozen examples of how speakin' the truth can get you killed. But it ain't as easy comin' up with town examples, where about the worst that can happen is hurtin' someone's feelin's. I try again: "Say you woke up this mornin' and my breath was God-awful. Would you tell me?"

"Yes."

"Okay. But then if you came to school and someone said, 'How's your father?' would you say, 'His breath smells like a bucket of armpits?'"

She giggles. "Maybe."

"Well, you shouldn't."

"Why?"

"'Cause people have feelin's, and them feelin's should be respected. It's the only way a town—or any group of people—can live together, with a certain style of life."

"I have no idea what you mean, Papa."

"If you and Miss Gilmore lived together in a sod house fifty miles from civilization you could probably call her Jean, or anythin' else, and she'd be happy for the conversation. But what works for two people, all alone in the world, don't work the same when there's a whole community of folks."

"Why not?"

"Because people judge each other based on how they're talked about."

She thinks about that a minute, but don't comment. So I say, "Your ma don't like you to say bad words in the house."

"Or anywhere else."

"Right."

"But *you* do," she says.

"Yes I do. Sometimes. I mean, I try hard not to, but I'm a rough man, in a hard business, and some of them I have to converse with don't necessarily respond to the King's English. Not that I'd know much about that type a' talkin' in the first place. Still, your ma and me want you to grow up better than we did. More refined. Lady-like. And proper ladies don't always tell the truth just because they know it. They know to hold back on sayin' things that might shock people, or hurt their feelin's."

"It hurts Miss Gilmore's feelin's that I'm a bastard?"

I sigh. "Callin' herself a bastard sounds to me like the kind of talk a very intelligent young lady might say to get attention."

She gives me a strange look, but I notice her ears startin' to turn red.

I say, "Though you're only five, or almost five, I s'pect you're the smartest person in town. That can't be easy for you, and I'm wonderin' if maybe you picked out Miss Gilmore as bein' the second smartest person in town. I wonder if maybe you're pickin' on her so she'll give you an entertainin' discussion, even if it gets your face slapped or your knuckles rapped. And I think there might be a part of you that hopes she'll argue 'stead of strikin' you 'cause you want to prove you're smarter than she is."

Scarlett lowers her eyes, says nothin'.

"You're a special girl, Scarlett, smartest I ever seen or heard of. But it takes more than brains to be happy. We have to build relationships with them we live amongst, and build friendships with them we care about. People will like you for bein' smart, long as you don't feel the need to *prove* how smart you are."

"I don't have any friends anyway," she says in a sorrowful voice.

"Everyone in Texas respects the cactus," I say. "But it's a rare person who'll hug one."

"What's that mean?"

"It means you've got a prickly way about you."

"Rose says it's my nature."

"Well, it still don't mean you can't have friends. Take a lesson from Rose's name: roses have thorns for protection, but also beautiful blooms that make people happy. What I'm sayin', it's okay to show you can protect yourself, but you'll have a happier life if you show your beautiful side as well."

"I'll try, Papa."

"Good. So even though it's true you're a bastard, and can talk like the smartest adults, predict the future, talk to snakes, and heal people—"

"I don't have to tell them all the things I can do."

"That's right."

"What if I know someone's doing something wrong?"

"You should keep it to yourself unless it involves danger."

"What kind of danger? Hurt feelings?"

"No. I'm talkin' about things like if you knew someone was gonna start a fire, or bully someone, or rob a bank, or kill a person."

"Okay."

"You understand?"

"Yes. You're saying I shouldn't tell people Mr. Way has been fornicating with Miss Gillmore."

"Exac—*What?*"

"Never mind."

"You're *sure* about that?"

"Never mind."

"But—"

"They're not starting a fire, Papa, or bullying, or robbing a bank, or killing anyone, so I'm not to say."

"When has this been takin' place? At night? Noon? In the mornin'?"

"You're trying to trick me. It won't work."

"But—"

"Look, Papa!" she says, suddenly excited.

I turn around and see Rose approachin'.

Scarlett races across the schoolyard to hug her.

CHAPTER 10

I MAKE MY way to where Rose and Scarlett are huggin' and right away Rose notices my limp.

"I leave for the shortest time and you're already hurt," she says. She looks at Scarlett. "Why haven't you done something about this?"

"I have. It was broken at first."

"It *was*?" That's news to me.

Rose says, "Can you get your boot off?"

"I doubt it."

"Okay. Sit."

I look around. "You mean right here? On the ground? In the middle of the whole town?"

"Don't be flamboyant. There are ten people at most who'll see you pushing my rump."

Scarlett laughs and claps her hands with delight at the thought of me pushin' Rose's backside with my foot.

"Well," I say, "I won't take pleasure in it."

"That's a pity," Rose says. "I have a fine backside, and few men get to brace against it. Now sit."

I do, then remove the boot from my good foot. Rose turns around and straddles my leg while holding the bottom of my boot. I take my good foot and push it against her butt.

"Harder," she says.

I look around and notice people have stopped to watch, point, and laugh.

I push harder, and when the boot finally comes off it only does so with great pain. Rose sets the boot down, inspects my ankle, and smiles. "Why, you've done a fine job, Scarlett!"

"I tried again this morning and all during the day, but he's still limping."

"That's because you didn't set the bone first."

Rose looks me in the eye and says, "We'll do that now."

I say, "Whoa. You don't mean to tell me you're plannin' to re-break my *ankle?*"

"Look on it as an opportunity to show Scarlett how brave and strong you are."

Scarlett's lookin' at me with anxious eyes. "Is it going to hurt really bad?" she asks.

Rose shows an evil grin. "It's going to hurt like a *bastard.*"

Scarlett's jaw drops. She covers her mouth and giggles.

I show Rose my deepest frown before sayin', "I don't know how you heard our conversation, but surely you can't object to Scarlett havin' bad language rules when it comes to livin' among town folk."

"I'm not opposed to certain rules. But you often do a pitiful job of explaining them."

"How would *you* explain 'em?"

She looks at Scarlett. "Honey, always tell town people what they want to hear. They're stupid, like cows, but dangerous, like bulls. Don't frighten them unless they're trying to burn you."

Scarlett smiles.

"You two are quite the pair," I say. Then scream, as Rose resets my half-healed ankle. Afterward, I say, "How am I supposed to get home on this leg?"

Rose points to the horse five feet behind me. It's my own mustang, Sally. And she's saddled. I'm usually good at hearin' animals come up behind me, but reckon I screamed so loud I missed this one. Rose and Shrug help me to my feet, and onto Sally's back, which forces me to wonder where Shrug came from, since I didn't hear *him* come up on me, neither.

On the way home I learn Rose got to Dodge an hour ago, met Gentry at the *Spur*, and the two of 'em went home and finished packin' Scarlett's things. Rose wants to leave immediately, figurin' to make twenty miles before settin' camp, which ought to put her and Scarlett in Saint Jo by noon tomorrow, which was her long-standin' plan.

"What's so all-fired important about gettin' to Saint Jo before noon tomorrow?" I ask.

"We've got a full schedule," Rose says.

"You never said exactly what sort a' things you're gonna teach her the next two weeks."

Scarlett and Rose give each other a look. Then Scarlett says, "Secret things."

"*Sacred* things," Rose corrects.

"Sacred things," Scarlett repeats.

"What type a' sacred things?" I ask. "Do I want to know?"

"No, you do not," Rose says. "Nor would you understand."

The two of 'em talk in snake tongue the rest of the way home, leavin' me to talk to Shrug, which I do till I realize he's no longer with us.

"When did Shrug leave?" I say, feelin' silly.

They don't answer. They're too busy chatterin' like magpies.

Or snakes, I should say.

That night, after Rose and Scarlett leave; after Gentry and I have a surprisin'ly quiet supper; after we climb into bed; she turns her back to me. I remind her she said we were gonna make love so loud tonight as to disturb the neighbors and their dogs. She harumphs. This comes as a surprise to me, and a little off-puttin', under the circumstances. I mean, the whole point of lettin' Scarlett go was for me and Gentry to have some alone time and put the romance back into our lives.

Before long I hear her sleepin' softly, and remind myself how much I love her, and that the physical part is just one wheel on our marriage wagon, but it don't help as much as I hoped, 'cause it's late, and my foot hurts, and I was all geared up for romance. I sigh, close my eyes, and try to fall asleep.

For some reason, my thoughts instantly go to Penelope, so I force 'em elsewhere, and that puts an end to it.

For about ten seconds.

Then they're back on Penelope with a vengeance.

I'm specifically tryin' not to think of her doe eyes, her poutin' lips, or the way her breath comes at me sweet and hot. Tryin' not to think about what she said to me, or how her hips sway gracefully when she walks.

But no matter how hard I try not to think about Penelope, she keeps workin' her way back into my thoughts. It's a complete mystery to me, 'cause why on earth would I think of Penelope while lyin' in bed with the prettiest, most wonderful woman I ever laid eyes on?

Is it 'cause Penelope wants me tonight and Gentry don't?

I certainly love Gentry with all my heart, and have no desire to lose her or give her up, but another thing I can't get out of my mind is how she kept sayin' Penelope's the only woman she fears I'd leave her for. There must be somethin' awful special about Penelope for Gentry to say that...and I wonder what it is.

After an hour of tossin' and turnin', and bein' as totally unsatisfied and full of heat as any man can be who's lyin' inches away from the most desirable woman on Earth, I wonder if maybe the thing that's extra special about Penelope is what she herself said to me this afternoon: that she'd never deny me, and always want me, and that she's always thinkin' about touchin' me. Touchin' me and dreamin' about us bein' together, her with no clothes on, and touchin' me and....

"*Emmett!* What on *earth?!!*"

"Huh?"

"Good *Lord!*"

"What? *Oh!* Uh...."

Gentry sits up. "I can't believe you *did* that! What *are* you, twelve?"

I take a deep breath, tell myself to stay quiet. I know she's startled, possibly angry from bein' woke up, and though I don't care for her attitude, or the fact she turned her back and harrumphed at me earlier, I'm hopin' this'll die down and be quick forgotten. If she says nothin' else on the matter I should be able to hold my tongue.

She feels around the bed with her hand. "Oh my *God!*" she says. "That's *disgusting!*"

"*Really*, Gentry? It's *disgustin'* to you?" I say, immediately wishin' I hadn't.

"What's *that* supposed to mean, Emmett? Are you saying that because I'm a whore I shouldn't be disgusted when my own husband pleasures himself in my bed?"

"You ain't a whore, Gentry."

"Of course I am. Once a whore, whore for life. I can only wonder what you must've been thinking about, lying there in the dark with your eyes closed. Not to mention *who* you were thinking about."

I say, "Let's just go back to sleep before we say things we don't mean."

"What if I say what I *do* mean?"

"This probably ain't a good time to—"

"Who *were* you thinking about just now? Certainly not *me*. I'm right here beside you."

"You're beside me, all right, but showin' no interest."

"I'm sorry I'm tired, Emmett. I'm sure most wives would have no problem sleeping last night if their husband brought a gut-shot gambler home and their daughter got mad and blew his head off! I'm sorry I didn't think to sleep all day so I'd be fresh enough to give you your poke instead of making your breakfast, working all day, coming home to pack Scarlett's things, and cook your dinner! I'm sorry I'm supposed to spread my legs every time you get an urge, even though our daughter's out in a field somewhere with a witch who puts Victoria's secrets to shame."

"Victoria? Who's that?"

She takes a deep breath. "The Queen of England, Emmett."

"She's got secrets?"

"Not as many as *you*, I expect."

"I don't have any secrets, Gentry."

"Then who were you thinking about just now?"

"I weren't thinkin' of no one. Sometimes it does a fella good to pull on it, that's all."

"That may be the first lie you ever told me. But no matter. I have a pretty good idea which little tramp has been on your mind."

"Who?"

"Just...go to sleep, Emmett. Assuming you've finished pulling on it for the night. And thanks a lot."

"For what?"

"For marrying me when you were in love with someone else."

"What the hell are you *talkin'* about? I love *you*, Gentry. No one else."

"Then prove it."

"How?"

"Judge the beauty contest."

"*What?* That's *crazy!*"

"Is it?"

"How's that gonna prove I love you?"

"I'm curious to see who you'll pick."

"If I'm stuck judgin' a beauty contest, there ain't but one woman I'd pick to win, and that's you."

"You can't pick me."

"Why not?"

"I'm your wife. It wouldn't be fair for me to enter."

"Well, that's fine, 'cause I ain't judgin' no stupid beauty contest in the first place."

"You will if you give a damn about Dodge."

"That don't make sense."

"You of all people should know how important this has become."

"What's *that* supposed to—"

"It's going to be the biggest event in the history of Dodge. It's all anyone's talking about. People are sending word from 50 miles away they wouldn't miss it for the world. This contest will put Dodge on the map. Newspapers all over the country will cover it. You should get on your knees and thank John Boone for coming up with the idea, but no, you'd rather criticize the idea and call it stupid, and refuse to participate."

"Tell me again why it is you want me to judge this…contest?"

"It's good for the town."

"What's the other part? The one about bein' curious who I pick."

"I assume you'll choose the woman you think is the prettiest one in the territory."

"No problem. If I can't pick you, I'll pick Scarlett."

"She won't be entering, either."

"Then I'll pick Rose."

"Sorry. No Rose. But don't despair. You'll still have the opportunity to gawk at every woman within fifty miles of Dodge. Oh, I *do* wonder who you'll choose. And who you won't."

"What's *that* mean?"

"I honestly don't know if you've already got a sweetheart, Emmett, but if you *do*, and don't pick her because you're afraid the whole territory will know who you've been poking, it'll affect her. As a woman I can tell you she'll never get over it, regardless of the reason."

"Just like you never got over me pickin' Leah over you in the White River nipple contest?"

"That's right, Emmett," she says, with ice in her voice. "Thanks for reminding me."

She gathers up her bedclothes, stands, and says, "Have fun pulling your pecker in a cold bed."

She goes to Scarlett's room, closes the door. I wait a few minutes, struggle to my feet, try to walk; but the pain in my foot's too strong. I want to go to her, tell her I love her, and put things back to normal. I know if I don't put an end to this argument tonight, things'll be worse in the mornin'. And if our distance keeps growin' more than a day or two, we might never get back where we were.

I slide, shuffle, and hop my way to Scarlett's room, but don't knock on the door.

I really want to...but my pride won't let me.

It was embarrassin' earlier, when she said all them things about catchin' me half asleep, doin' what I was doin'. Didn't seem to matter I only done it 'cause she wouldn't do *her* job.

I sigh.

That didn't come out right. I know it ain't her job to satisfy me, but what I'm thinkin', she made the offer *last* night, and I'd been lookin' forward to it. Also, she never hesitated cuddlin' up to me before. Or maybe it's just that *I* didn't mind so much when she didn't give up her charms in the past, 'cause it weren't as important to me before.

What made it important tonight?

I wanted reassurance.

Penelope painted a fantastical portrait of romantic love this afternoon, but it weren't any different than the type of relationship me and Gentry used to have before speakin' our marriage vows. But lately there's been less romance. Not just the kind that takes place under the covers, but also that fun way of talkin' we used to share, and the secret looks we gave when we knew we both wanted the same amount of affection. In them days the smiles and laughs and hugs made us constantly yearn to be together. When we were forced apart the hours seemed like days, and when we came back together we'd melt into each other's arms and become two parts of the same person. We slept with passion and woke up contented, with the kind of blissful joy that made us burst with happiness. But since we ain't been that way for months I was hopin' with Scarlett out of the house Gentry might show she wants to couple up with me as much as Penelope wants to. I think if Gentry had been excited about us bein' alone in the house, 'stead of bein tired and worried about Scarlett, she'd have given me her charms and I'd have forgotten all about Penelope and her foolish talk.

But now I'm wonderin' if Gentry's grown tired of me.

It's not just possible, it's likely, since I'm almost twice her age. She's bound to wish I was younger. Can I really blame her if she don't want to cuddle up to a man who's old enough to be her father? On the other hand, Penelope's only two years older than Gentry, which means I'm almost twice as old as *she* is, too. And somehow *she* don't seem to find me the least bit unattractive.

Or disgustin'.

Gentry didn't come right out and say I disgusted her tonight. She *did* say the word, but I'm pretty sure she was talkin' not about *me*, but my behavior. Now that I think on it, this probably ain't the first time I disgusted her since we've been a couple. It's probably just the first time she said it out loud.

The hurtful words she said ain't the type a man wants to hear after givin' up his way of life in the woods, mountains, and prairies to make a happier home for his wife and daughter.

Not that a prissy, city gal like Penelope would want to live off the land, either. But maybe she'd be a little more grateful over how well she's been loved and treated.

I turn around and trudge back to our bedroom, close the door, and lie awake another hour, worryin' about my future with Gentry, and thinkin' how awful life would be if our special way of livin' continues fadin' further and further into the past. I decide then and there that keepin' Gentry's the most important thing in the world. She's everythin' to me, and so I make a solemn vow to never allow thoughts of another woman to enter my brain for as long as I live.

After makin' that commitment, I feel like the weight of the world has been lifted from my shoulders. I finally fall asleep, and have the most amazin' dream of my life.

Unfortunately, the dream is about Penelope, and—as she predicted—she ain't wearin' clothes.

What I don't understand is how vivid the dreams are. In my whole life I never dreamed these types of details about *anythin'*, let alone a woman's body. It's as if she's in the house with me at high noon, in a room with no roof, and no part of her body hidden by shade or shadow. I see every cut, bruise, mark, or scrape. Every mole and freckle. I can even *smell* her.

I wake up stiff as a stallion, ready to rut.

But Gentry ain't in the room.

CHAPTER 11

MY FIRST SURPRISE is my ankle, and how I'm able to put my weight on it. I'm limpin', but less so than yesterday mornin'.

My second surprise is Gentry, who don't seem to care if my ankle's better, and even worse, she don't seem to notice me at all. I apologize to her for last night and tell her I hope we can patch things up today.

When she don't respond I ask, "How could things get so bad between us last night that you won't speak to me today?"

"You said enough last night."

I ain't sure what she means till she says, "Your actions spoke louder than words. What you did spoke volumes."

"About what?"

"Our marriage."

I frown and say, "It can't be that strange for an unsatis-fied man to pull his pecker once in a blue moon."

"Oh, really? Well, I suppose I should thank you for that."

"For what?"

"Sharing how you feel."

"What do you mean?"

"I hadn't realized how unsatisfied you've been all this time."

"All *what* time?"

She says nothin'.

"I was just talkin' about last *night*," I say. "That's the only night I was unsatisfied."

I didn't realize till just now that all this time she's been packin' *her* lunch, but not mine. I watch her put hers in her carpetbag to take to the *Spur*.

"Gentry?"

She don't answer. Just keeps movin' about the house, frosty as a snowman.

Now that I'm in a mood to notice, I see she ain't made breakfast for either of us.

As she's puttin' her shawl on I say, "Where you goin' this early?"

"To work, Emmett."

"Without breakfast?"

She says nothin'.

When she heads for the door I say, "Am I to make my own breakfast and lunch today?"

She stops, looks me square in the face and says, "I as-sumed you had enough pies and cookies in your office to last a week. As for conversation, if that's what you desire, I expect you can get it from the stampede of women marching in and out of your office." She takes a deep breath, then says, "I'm certain one or more of them will be glad to pull your pecker, should you continue to find yourself so thoroughly unsatisfied."

With that, she storms out the door and slams it behind her without offerin' so much as a goodbye.

As I watch her from the window I think about John Boone, and wonder if I should remind Gentry that the sheriff's wife is supposed to feed the prisoners.

CHAPTER 12

LIMPIN' THROUGH TOWN I see four women marchin' back and forth in front of my office with signs that say:

> *Free John Boone!*
> *Let Our Dentist Go!*
> *Set John Free!*
> And, *John Done Us a Favor!*

I ain't in the mood for additional female confrontation, so I turn and head the opposite direction, toward the livery where my first wife, Amy, works, takin' care of Jim Bigsby's stock in return for room and board. It ain't meant to be a permanent job, but Jim and his wife, Clara, were willin' to help provide for her till I finish buildin' her house. I ain't *personally* buildin' it, just payin' the carpenters from Saint Jo to do so. Unfortunately, they're swamped with other local projects, and Amy's house ain't likely to be started for at least two months.

"Hey, Amy."

"Emmett."

"I come to check on you."

"Thanks. I'm okay."

"You sure?"

She gestures at the hay around her. "It's not paradise, but I'm not a complainer."

"If anyone has a right to complain, it'd be you."

That's the truth if ever it was spoken. While Amy ain't as hard a woman to look at as Ella Foreskin, her face is non-stop scars, busted teeth, and a nose that looks like someone broke a teapot and dumped the pieces in a cow patty. There are patches of hair missin' from her scalp. Her arms are permanently puckered and glazed from burns. Still, if you were lookin' at her right now as she works on Jim's bay mare with a wire brush, you'd be able to tell she was pretty once upon a time.

She catches me starin', and says, "I noticed you're limping."

"A wagon caught fire and fell on my foot."

She nods. "I heard about that. But I think maybe something else is bothering you."

Though she ain't said much for a woman, it occurs to me this is the most conversation I've heard out of Amy since the Dog Soldiers traded her back to civilization for some Henry rifles.

"Why the sad face, Emmett?" she prods.

There ain't too many people I'd tell my troubles to, but Amy and I were childhood sweethearts, and in them days she was always a good listener. She and I are still paperwork married, since I ain't yet found a judge to divorce us proper. That's one of the things that's been stickin' in Gentry's craw these past months, though the way she phrased it was she'd love to be my *only* legal wife. At least, that's how she felt *before* last night. At the moment I ain't sure what to think about Gentry's feelin's toward me.

I sigh.

"Emmett?"

I look at Amy and shrug. Though I decided not to speak about it, the words come tumblin' out my mouth: "Gentry and me ain't as romantical as we used to be, and I have to judge a beauty contest that'll make everyone in town angry 'cept the winner's family."

"What else?" she says.

"My prisoner, John Boone, shot a pervert. The town women want me to release him 'cause we need a dentist and he *is* one, but the law's the law, so I sent a report to Wichita, and they'll probably make me take him there, or somewhere else, to be tried for murder."

"What else?"

I think a moment. "That's about it."

She nods.

I say, "Got any advice for me?"

"I'm at a loss for words."

"How come?"

"*These* are your earth-shattering problems, Emmett? Your wife stopped *poking* you? You have to judge a *beauty* contest? You're being forced to do the job for which you're *paid?*"

I think about it. "Yup. That's about it."

She laughs. "And all this time I thought *I* had troubles."

I never asked Amy what it was like livin' among the Dog Soldiers, who I consider the fiercest, most undisciplined renegades in the West. I didn't ask because I didn't want to force her to relive memories she'd rather forget. I figured if she wanted to talk about them lost years she'd do so, when the time was right. But since she brought it up just now, this seems a good time to ask, "What's troubling *you*, Amy?"

She continues brushing the bay's chest and underbelly. When she gets to the forelegs she says, "Do you *really* want to know, or are you just being polite?"

"Both. But I'm definitely keen to hear as much as you're comfortable sayin'.""

She says, "I hesitate to speak of troubles because I don't wish to appear ungrateful for all you've done. I know I've put you in a difficult situation, showing up on your doorstep after all these years."

"I'm glad you're alive, Amy. Truth is, your bein' here's a lot harder on Gentry than me."

She works in silence, so I say, "How are things workin' out with Jim and Clara?"

"You don't know?"

"What?"

"I've been moved out of the house."

"*What?* Where are you *sleepin'?*"

"Here. In the straw, amidst the horse shit."

"Since when?"

"Since Clara caught Jim fucking me."

"What?"

"Don't act like you didn't know."

"I don't know anything about this."

She frowns. "It's the arrangement *you* set up with him. He agreed to give me room and board, and in return I'd fuck him and tend to his stock."

"There weren't nothin' in the arrangement I made with Jim that involved fuckin'."

She stops brushin' the horse a minute, looks at me, then smiles a sad smile. "Well, I suppose that proves how little I expect from men."

The more I think on it, the angrier I get. "Jim forced himself on you?"

"It would serve him right if I said yes, but I can't claim what isn't so. Jim reached out to touch me so casually that first night I assumed it was part of the arrangement. I didn't even think to stop him. After what I've been through, believe me, it was nothing. Of course, now that I'm sleeping in the barn, things have...."

She closes her eyes, allows her words to float away, as if to some far off place. But I can't let them go unsaid.

"Things have what?"

"Never mind. I shouldn't have said that."

"I'd like to hear what you were about to say."

She sighs. "Let's not make too much of it. You've got troubles enough without adding mine to the pot."

"I'd like to help."

"You're already building me a house. By the way, I plan to pay you back for that, eventually."

"There's no need, Amy. It's somethin' me and Gentry want to do for you."

She looks at me through moist eyes. "Thank you, Emmett. I appreciate that more than I can express. The promise of having a home someday is a huge thing. I don't want to get my hopes up too high over it actually happening, but...it's a huge thing to hope for. It wouldn't be fair to burden you with any of my complaints."

"It's okay, I want to hear 'em. And if you're willin', I'd also like to hear your story."

"Don't you have some sheriffing to do?"

"Yeah, but it'll keep."

"What about Gentry? Won't she be upset if someone tells her we were talking a long time?"

"Probably. How 'bout you give me the short version?"

She laughs. "Okay. Brief history: I was fourteen when we married, and I loved you with all my heart. That was 1849."

I nod.

She says, "What year is it now?"

"You don't know?"

She shakes her head. "I tried to count them, and came up with fifteen. Is that right?"

"You're close. It's 1866. Closin' in on 1867."

She stares into space before sayin', "So anyway...we'd been married five or six weeks when the Masikotas attacked our little settlement. You and most of the men were off hunting the Cheyenne who killed your parents and the others."

"The Masikotas killed everyone but you."

She says, "They killed a few and burned the others and made me watch every bit of it."

"They burned 'em alive?"

I hadn't realized that.

She nods. "I can still smell it. It'll be with me forever, the screams...the scent of burning flesh on the roasted bodies that used to be our friends and neighbors...." She stares into space and says, "The only warriors that didn't rape me were the ones standing lookout. Then, when the others were done, the lookouts took their turn. I don't know how many participated in all, because most of them took more than one run at me, and it went on for hours. Fortunately, I was unconscious half the time, since they beat me practically senseless."

She pauses. "They raped me every way a woman can be raped. Did things to me I didn't even know could be done. Remember, I was only fourteen."

We're quiet till she says, "For years there was hardly a day I wasn't beaten or raped, or used as a human outhouse, or otherwise humiliated. I was passed around to every warrior from every tribe that visited our camp. Over the years every squaw in the tribe led her sons to the place they kept me staked, and watched them rut me as a rite of passage. I birthed at least two babies before my insides were completely destroyed, but they were taken away and taught to hate me. Had I lived with the tribe long enough, they would have made my own sons rut me in their eleventh year."

"How'd you wind up with the Dog Soldiers?"

She coughs out a laugh. "The Masikotas traded me for a dead donkey and a sack of salt. At the time I was foolish enough to think my life could only get better, but that hope ended within' hours, when the Dog Soldiers taught me the true meaning of evil."

"What did *they* do to you?"

"You wouldn't believe it if I told you."

"I'm truly sorry, Amy."

She waves off my words with her hand and says, "So anyway, they eventually got tired of rutting me, carving me up, and making me do things with their goats and horses, so they traded me to Sadie Nickers, and here I am."

"Well, maybe things are finally looking up for you."

"Yes. Until recently I had the good fortune to live with Jim and Clara, and work here, in the stable. I still get to work and sleep here, but these days it's less food and no pay and I've still continued to rut your friend daily."

I look around the stable. "This ain't no place for a woman."

She smiles. "Dear Emmett, if only all men were more like you. But listen: yes, this stable is filthy, smelly, and the roof leaks unmercifully, but it's paradise compared to how I used to live. And two people have been a godsend: your friend Wayne, and your daughter."

"What about my daughter?"

"I'm sure I don't have to tell you she has healing powers."

"I've heard others claim it," I say.

"Well, Wayne brought me rag soup, and your daughter heals me from a distance."

"I didn't know Scarlett was doin' that."

"Please thank her for me, as I've thanked Wayne. Without them, I'd be in bad shape."

"Why's that?"

"Lately a gang of men have been coming for me at night."

"What do you mean?"

"They hold me down, beat me, gang-rape me."

"*What*? Which men?"

"I don't know. It's always dark, and they wear hoods, so I only know them by their voices and personal smells." You know how Masikotas can smell the difference between white men? I can do that, too."

"I'd heard that about Masikotas, but I doubt your smell testimony will stand up in court."

"It doesn't matter. Compared to what I'm used to, it's not that bad. And these town men are beginning to realize they don't need to beat me if I'm not fighting back. Still, they're aggressive enough that without Scarlett's healing, I'd have a hard time getting my work done."

"Does Jim know about the men?"

She shrugs. "Probably not. But if he did, he wouldn't lift a finger to stop them."

"I noticed some bruises and cuts, but figured they were from workin' with stubborn horses." I study her face a minute, then say, "Except that small one above your right eye that looks like a dot in a circle, like a target."

She shrugs. "I'm not sure what you're referring to, as I make it a point to avoid mirrors."

"What I'm sayin', your injuries don't match what you just described."

"I have Scarlett to thank for that happy result. Every night the men brutalize me, and every day she heals me as best she can."

"If she *hadn't* healed you I expect others would've noticed your condition and brought it to my attention."

"Don't worry about it. Someday, thanks to you, I'll have a nice home, and be less vulnerable to rapists."

"I got an idea. I'll put you in John Boone's room at the hotel till your house is built."

She smiles. "That's a noble thought, but you'd better rethink that. The town women will talk."

"About what?"

"They'll say I'm your kept woman."

"I'll put you there anyway."

"When?"

"Right now. Get your things together."

She laughs. "Did you really just say that?"

What she means is she ain't got any "things" to get together except the filthy rags she's wearin'.

"Amy, I've done you wrong these past months."

"How so?"

"I purposely avoided checkin' in on you 'cause I didn't want to upset Gentry. But I intend to do better, startin' today. I'm gonna end this stable arrangement you got with Jim Bigsby, get you cleaned up, buy you some new clothes, and make sure the hotel feeds you three meals a day."

"You don't have to do all that, Emmett. I'm willing to earn my keep. I can't whore at your saloon, because of Gentry, but I could entertain gentlemen callers at the hotel, for a fee, and pass it on to you."

"We can talk about that later. Right now I aim to get you in a clean, safe place, and give you time to mend."

I don't want Amy whorin' for me or anyone else. I only said we could talk about it later 'cause I don't want her to think she's gettin' too much charity. It ain't that I got an is-sue with whorin', but the sad truth is Amy's unusable as a town whore. I doubt there's a man in Kansas who'd pay Amy two bits for a poke, though she might fetch that much at a hog ranch.

I sigh, wonderin' what's to become of my first wife. I'll make sure she survives, and has a home, but women need more than shelter to be happy. They need friendship, and love, if they can get it.

As we head to the hotel I come up short tryin' to figure what woman in this town might want to be Amy's friend. Gentry's kind enough to do it, but it'd be awfully hard on her, since Amy and me are still legally married, and Gentry's already bein' teased about it. As for the proper women, well, they'd never consort with her due to the gruesome scars all over her face, and because of the immoral life they feel she's led. Even the whores will keep shunnin' her, same as they've done since the day she arrived, since they consider white squaws to be the lowest members of society.

Up to now I thought Jim and Clara were her friends, but Jim's ruined that. I s'pect Clara thinks Amy's the culprit, and I can see why: out of the goodness of her heart, Clara gave Amy a place to stay, a job to work, and fed her three times a day, only to catch her pokin' her husband. I think of poor Clara, dyin' of consumption, havin' to deal with Jim's infidelity with a sorrowful heart, thinkin' Amy betrayed her kindness. Noble Clara, not tellin' anyone in town what Jim and Amy done. If she had told a soul, I'd have heard about it, 'cause there ain't many secrets in this town that don't come to light in short order.

Unfortunately things are only gonna get worse for Amy when I find the men who've been rapin' her, 'cause they're either young men or married men, and their mothers or wives will wind up blamin' Amy, and say she led 'em on. When I punish these men, Amy'll be talked about, pointed at, and probably much worse. She'll be a victim all over again.

"I'm real sorry about all this, Amy. I'll make it right, if I can."

"Thank you, Emmett."

"I should a' done more."

"Emmett?"

"Yeah?"

"No matter how bad things get, I'll handle it, and hold my head high."

"I believe you will."

Now, after makin' all the arrangements, and gettin' her settled into the room, and seein' how she gawked at the furniture in amazement, and how she kept starin' out the window with tears in her eyes, I can't help but think if I was judgin' a beauty contest today, I'd give Amy the prize despite her pitiful appearance.

CHAPTER 13

BY THE TIME I get back to my office the sign-carryin' women have gone home. I ain't surprised. Pioneerin' requires a dawn-to-dusk effort, seven days a week, and these Philadelphia sign-carriers probably realized pretty quick there weren't many people on the streets to take notice. I figure John Boone'll be starvin' by now, so I put a slice of pie and some cookies on a plate and carry it into the back room, and am shocked to find May Gray standin' in front of Boone's cell with her tits hangin' out!

"What's this?" I say.

May's facin' me, and her back's against the cell. John's behind her with his hands around her neck. She wants to move away, but John's grip is too tight. She has free use of her hands, and was makin' every effort to pull his hands from her neck when I come through the door just now, but at the moment she's attemptin' to cover her nakedness with 'em, though I've seen this particular set of titties once before.

John says, "Release me now, Sheriff, or I'll crush her neck."

The napkin and fried chicken remnants on his cot, and crumbs on the floor, tell me they'd been havin' a grand little picnic and party till they heard me enter the outer office. I reckon that's when John spun May around and grabbed her by the throat.

"*Now*, Sheriff!" he says.

I produce my gun and place it beside his ear. "Let her go or I'll shoot you."

"You wouldn't dare!"

After tellin' May to put her fingers in her ear, I lower the gun and shoot the heel off the bottom of his boot. He wobbles, releases his grip, and she falls to the floor.

I look at May. "Better tuck 'em back in your dress before half the town comes runnin' to see what I was shootin' at."

As she does so, quite red-faced, she says, "I trust I can count on your discretion."

"I ain't sure what that means."

"It means don't tell anyone what happened."

"I don't know how that's possible. I mean, they'll know I didn't fry no chicken."

"Tell them I brought the prisoner some food, he ate it, then tried to choke me to death."

I nod slowly. "Okay. I can tell that much with a clear conscience."

Boone says, "That takes care of the sheriff, but what about me?"

"What *about* you?" she says, indignantly.

"I'll expect another visit if you want to buy my silence."

"*What?* That's an *outrage!*"

"Your choice," he says, "but make it now. I've already seen what you've got. I'll describe them in precise detail to anyone who cares to listen, which I assume will be the entire town."

"Sheriff?" she says, lookin' to me for help.

I turn my palms up. "I ain't sure what you want from me. I don't have to tell everythin' I saw, but if he tells people you shared your charms I won't be able to deny it."

"You're going to allow him to...to..."

"It seems to me you already allowed him to do what he's askin'."

People are hollerin' outside the jail house wall, takin' a cautious approach, askin' if everyone's okay inside.

"We're fine!" I holler. "Stay where you are, I'll be right out." I turn to John Boone and say, "What exactly are we talkin' about?"

"I want twenty minutes with her naked body."

"That ain't gonna happen." I think a minute, then say, "If she's willin' to come back this afternoon I might allow you two minutes to touch 'em again, in a gentle manner. But that's as far as it goes."

"It'll go as far as I say it goes," Boone sneers.

May looks at me through frightened eyes.

I show Boone my hard stare and say, "I'm tryin' to bro-ker a fair trade here. Like you said, you already saw and touched 'em with her permission. If it'll buy your silence and preserve her dignity I'd call that a fair trade. Or I could do the easy thing and kill you right now, since the timin' will never be more perfect." I point my gun at his forehead. "I'll leave it up to you." I cock the hammer on my gun, fully intendin' to shoot him, as I don't like the man, nor his attitude toward women.

"Two minutes?" he says.

I look at May. "Will that work for you?"

She squeezes her eyes shut. Then nods.

"You've got yourself a deal," Boone says, "provided she shines a favorable light on my character when telling her story."

CHAPTER 14

THE SOUND OF a gun bein' fired is unmistakable. It's a sound every man, woman, and child in Kansas can immediately identify. At night, gun noise don't carry far, due to piano-playin', general hoorayin', and other types of commotion. But in the daytime there ain't many businesses or nearby homes that'd fail to hear a gunshot, even if fired indoors. And generally speakin', when guns are fired people want to know why. For this reason, I ain't surprised to see Penelope among the small crowd in front of my office, but I *am* surprised Gentry ain't here. I see Jim Bigsby, and wonder if he's here because of the shot or because I moved Amy out of his stable.

The folks waitin' to hear from me ain't exactly nervous, 'cause minutes ago they heard me holler out things were fine. But they're cat-curious as to why I told 'em to wait outside.

What I notice more than anything else is the relief I see in Penelope's face. The tears in her eyes convince me she was genuinely worried for my safety, which moves me more than it probably should. But if that ain't enough, I see her silently mouth the words "Thank God," even though she's standin' by her husband's side as she says it.

She's makin' strong eye contact with me, but so are the other women, 'cause I'm about to make a public statement, and the nature of town women is to listen very closely to public statements. They'll focus on what I *don't* say, as well as what I *do*, and *how* I say it, so they can chatter endlessly about it over the next few days, and eventually mark it on their calendars as the day things forever changed in Dodge, assumin' something happens in the future that makes to-day's shootin' seem particularly relevant.

Like how this event changed May Gray's life forever, un-less I can keep that from happenin'.

I have a certain fondness for May, and respect how she raised three capable young ladies on her own, and got through the war without losin' her pride, or her prized gar-den. While it's true her father shipped her a steady stream of supplies durin' the war years, I've seen lots of families do far less with far more.

Before the war, when people died in town it often fell to May's husband to haul the bodies to Fort Dodge so the soldiers could bury 'em, on account of the whole county not havin' a good enough pick or shovel to dig grave-deep in this hard dirt. In the dark of night before the haulin' com-menced, May would strip the dead of all usable clothin' and through the magic of her soap and sewin' needles, managed to turn the nastiest, filthiest clothes into dresses, night-gowns, quilts, and curtains you'd swear were ordered from the finest stores back East. Durin' the war she was known for sharin' her food and supplies with the town widows, and for keepin' herself and her girls fresh-scrubbed. Her husband's death left a hole in May's life she's been keen to fill, and it's this deep desire for a husband that's made her quick to show her titties of late: to *me* two years ago and to John Boone today. She's a good woman, if desperate, and I aim to preserve her reputation as best I can without tellin' any lies.

My office doorstep puts me a foot higher than the tallest folks who have gathered to hear me tell what happened. The announcement should be quick and simple, but I'm only wearin' one gun, and Shrug ain't in town to help back me up, should things get out of control. Reason I'm bringin' this up, I've seen curious crowds turn to angry mobs at the drop of a hat, and know full well there ain't no sure bets about the outcome when sheriffs address town folk.

I'd also feel better if Gentry was here, but she still ain't showed. Then again, if anythin' were to go wrong I'd worry for her safety, 'cause Dodge is the type a' town where all men and some women carry guns and knives at all times. Sure, Gentry's upset with me, but I reckon she'd still care if I got shot. I expect the reason she ain't showed is she knows I can take care of myself, and she's probably keepin' a close eye on the *Spur*, to make sure no one robs the place or torments Rudy, our bear, when most of the town's people are a couple of blocks away.

Still, it ain't like her not to check on my safety when she hears a shot fired.

I don't know why these thoughts of Gentry cause me to glance at Penelope, but the moment I do, somethin' registers in her eyes. I don't know what she thinks she saw in my look, but she's suddenly workin' hard to hide a smile.

I frown, clear my throat, and say, "Thanks for comin', everyone. It's a good practice to check the source of any gunshots you hear, like you just did, though I recommend in the future you ladies find a safe place and stay removed from the line of fire."

"What happened?" someone hollers out.

"There ain't a whole lot to report. You all know May Gray. She was kind enough to bring food to my prisoner, John Boone, who used the opportunity to attempt an escape."

A couple of women gasp.

"Mr. Boone grabbed May by the throat, and threatened her life. I shot his boot heel out from under him to make him let go of her. And he did."

I let the crowd murmur on that till someone says, "What took you so long to come out and talk about it?"

"My first responsibility was to make sure May was fully recovered, which she is." With that, I turn and motion May to come forward. She does, and tells people not to judge John Boone harshly, as he's never been incarcerated before, and was suddenly overcome by panic over his grim situation.

She surprises me by goin' so far as to say, "I'm not sure why Emmett feels the need to take John to trial. I believe many of you feel as I do that he did the town a service by killing Eli Shed, who killed his wife and behaved improperly toward some of our school children. I agree Mr. Boone has responded poorly to captivity, but I wonder how many of us could handle being incarcerated 36 hours in a jail cell. I personally don't fault John for panicking. He grabbed at me the same way a drowning man would grab a lifeline. But can you really blame him? The crime Emmett's accusing him of calls for death by hanging, which would be a travesty, since in many ways I consider John Boone a hero for shooting Eli Shed."

By the time she gets that far in her speech, half the crowd's harumphin' and carryin' on, and the other half's sayin', "She's right, Sheriff!" and, "What about *that*, Emmett?"

Then May goes in for the kill, sayin', "I probably shouldn't tell this, but I have it on the highest possible authority that before he died, Eli Shed told Emmett he didn't want to press charges against Mr. Boone."

I hear more gasps from the crowd, and lots of loud murmurin'. May, gettin' into it, holds her hand up to quiet 'em down before sayin', "According to my most excellent reliable source, the reason Eli didn't want to press charges is because he felt Mr. Boone may have had cause to shoot him, and because the town is in dire need of a dentist."

For a second or two, everyone looks at each other. Then a bunch of 'em break into a chant: "Let him go! Let him go!" Others start chimin' in, with raised fists.

I look from one angry face to the next, wonderin' how I lost control of the situation so quickly. Then my eyes find Penelope's, and I feel the same way John Boone supposedly felt when he was grabbin' a lifeline. She gives me the faintest nod, and I give her one in return. It's like the two of us are connected somehow, the way me and Gentry used to be. I instinctively glance at her husband, Oliver, and notice him reachin' up to hold her arm, same as any lovin' husband might do in a situation that threatens to get out of hand.

Then someone—Jim Bigsby—shouts out the question to May I knew was comin': "Who told you all those things Eli said before he died?"

And May says, "Gentry Love."

All eyes turn to me, and everyone goes quiet.

I say, "May, I seriously doubt Gentry told you that, since you and her ain't particularly close. But she probably told someone, and that person told you."

"Is it true?" several people shout.

"It is. But like I told Gentry, it don't change things. This weren't no simple assault, where a victim can refuse to press charges. John Boone murdered Eli in cold blood. It don't matter that Eli turned out to be a bad person, 'cause John Boone didn't know that at the time. What I'm sayin', you can't go around shootin' people hopin' to discover they were bad people all along. And even if Boone *had* known what sort of things Eli was doin', it ain't up to him to take the law into his own hands."

I feel pleased with what I said, and figure everyone will agree, 'cause it's common sense. But them thoughts die quick when I see the crowd doublin' in size, and the men among 'em shakin' fists and makin' threatenin' gestures. The one that seems angriest is my old friend Jim Bigsby. I raise my left hand to divert the crowd's attention, then quick-draw my gun with my right hand, and shoot Penelope's husband in the foot.

CHAPTER 15

EVERYONE IN THE crowd is shocked, but none more so than Penelope, who gives up a loud scream. Of course, her husband Oliver is hollerin' fit to bust. He's rollin' around on the ground, cryin', grabbin' his foot. The men in the crowd ain't quite as angry as they were before the shot, but they ain't leavin', neither. Penelope and a couple of the women are tryin' to tend to Oliver, but he won't set still long enough to let 'em do much.

Penelope's close friend Amelia Evans looks up at me and demands, "What's the meaning of this?"

"I'm placin' Oliver Way under arrest."

"*What?*" Penelope says.

"On what charge?" Amelia says.

"Rape."

That quiets the crowd long enough for me to say, "I'll handle this. You folks need to go on about your business."

"Who'd he rape?" someone shouts.

"Amy Love," I say.

"That's preposterous!" Amelia says. She looks at Penelope. "*Tell* him!"

Penelope's eyes search mine. Then she says, "I doubt the sheriff would shoot anyone without proper cause."

Amelia's jaw drops.

Oliver stops hollerin' long enough to shout, "It's a lie! A bald-faced lie!"

"You'll get a chance to tell your side of the story," I say. "In the meantime, I'm puttin' you in a jail cell."

Someone remembers why he was mad a moment ago and shouts, "What about John Boone?"

"Yeah!" someone else says, "What about Boone?"

The crowd starts chantin', "What about Boone? What about Boone?"

I raise my left hand again, and this time everyone starts backin' up at a quick pace, tryin' to tuck their feet behind whoever's feet they're standin' beside, which causes most of 'em to trip and fall. They all roll about, tryin' to protect their feet from gettin' shot while I say, "Don't worry about John Boone. He'll get a fair trial. I sent a full report to Wichita yesterday afternoon, and included all details about what Boone did and what type of man Eli was. I said most of our citizens believe Boone should be released, and mentioned he's a dentist and we sorely need one here in Dodge. I expect to hear back from the judge in a matter of days. He'll probably put Boone on trial for murder, but might see his way to be lenient, since Boone ultimately done the town a service. Though he didn't shoot Eli to protect our kids, I believe our kids are safer than they were. Now please go on about your business, and trust me to do my job."

"Who took the report to Wichita?" Jim Bigsby asks.

"My friend Shrug."

"What about Oliver's foot?" Penelope says.

It suddenly strikes me I can't put Oliver in one of my jail cells, since I promised John Boone he could pet May's titties for two minutes later this afternoon. So I say, "If a couple of Oliver's friends will get him to the *Spur*, I'm sure Gentry will clean his wound. It ain't a bad one. At the most I shot the smallest tip off his little toe. Gentry'll pour some whiskey on it and sew it shut, and I'll collect Oliver in a little while." I look at May and say, "Before you leave, we need to fill out a report."

She nods.

I turn my attention to Penelope and say, "I'll need to ask you a few questions about Oliver."

Amelia says, "She should have an attorney with her before answering any questions."

"Why?"

"That's how it works in Philadelphia."

"Well that may be true, but here in Dodge it's the guilty one that needs an attorney."

Amelia says, "There should be a witness present during any questioning."

"Why?"

"To ensure that whatever information Penelope divulges is accurately recorded."

I do what I always do when I can't understand some-one's flowery language: frown. Then say, "She'll write her own statement, in her own hand, and sign it."

Amelia implores Penelope to secure an attorney before answerin' any questions or givin' any statements.

"Thanks Amelia," Penelope says. "But Emmett Love's integrity is legendary. If you'll remember, it's the primary reason we moved our homes and families to Dodge. And anyway, I'm certain this business with Oliver is a complete misunderstanding, and anything I say to the sheriff will only serve my husband's cause by proving his innocence. In any case, I trust Emmett to produce a faithful account of any-thing he and I discuss."

Jim Bigsby curls his lip at me and says, "You shot one of our most influential Philadelphians just now in front of more than twenty witnesses, and publicly branded him a rapist. Did you do that solely on the word of a white squaw?"

"You'd best tread lightly, Jim."

"Why's that, Emmett?" he sneers.

"Because I know Amy's word to be true, and would ar-rest any man on her say so. But in this situation I also have evidence that can't be refuted."

"What evidence is that?"

"You can come to the trial for those answers, if you like. And if you want to talk about anythin' else Amy told me, we can do that tonight, at your house."

He frowns.

"Sheriff?" Penelope says. "I know you'll want to ask me specific questions as soon as possible, but can we wait until I'm certain Oliver's properly cared for?"

"Yes, of course."

"Thank you. I'll come by after Gentry sews his toe."

I tip my hat, nod at the crowd, watch 'em slowly disburse. Then escort May into my office, and lock the door.

"I know we said this afternoon, but we'd better go ahead and get this done."

May takes a deep breath, then says, "Very well."

John Boone's lips curl into a wide grin. "You just couldn't wait, could you!"

May looks at me and says, "Thank you, sheriff. I'll trust you to come back in two minutes, as we agreed."

"We agreed there'd be two minutes of tittie play, but I never agreed to leave the two of you alone."

She looks shocked. "Surely you don't expect to—"

"I expect nothin', which is why I aim to stay. It's for your safety, May, and no other reason. I can't take a chance he won't strangle you again, or take advantage of the situation by goin' further than we agreed."

The look on her face tells me she understands why I need to be present, but she's mighty embarrassed about it, and says, "This is wrong on every level."

"You don't have to do it at all," I say. "It'll be your word against his."

Boone says, "That's right, May darling. But when I tell my version of events I'll also point out that Emmett Love knows I'm telling the truth. I expect they'll ask him which of us is lying."

May looks at me through pleadin' eyes.

I sigh. "I'm sorry about this, May. I can only promise I'll take no pleasure from watchin'."

She frowns. "I doubt that sincerely."

Boone says, "Enough talk. Show me those hairy gorilla tits and start the clock!"

CHAPTER 16

Five minutes later...

I DON'T KNOW which of us was more embarrassed durin' them two minutes, me or May Gray, but once the clock started, John Boone went to work on her naked bosoms like nothin' I ever saw. He set 'em to flappin' and billowin' like bed sheets in a tornado, and made sounds I wouldn't expect to hear from this type of activity, nor any other. Nor were they sounds I'd ever heard in town, nor in the wildest forests, nor the vastest wildernesses of nature. Nor were they sounds I'd want to hear again. As the seconds dragged on, May shuddered and gasped, her head pitched from side to side, and her legs buckled more than once. But through it all she stood her ground as brave as any soldier who's made his peace, knowin' his situation is helpless, after the last line of defense has been overrun by overwhelmin' enemy forces.

By the time I called out the two-minute mark Boone had consumed her udders as thoroughly as quicksand ever consumed a helpless horse. When May realized it was finally over, she stepped back, staggered, and fell into my arms as exhausted and spent as if she'd given birth to the devil, after twelve hours of labor.

The goodbyes were as awkward as any I've experienced, and now, watchin' May headin' down the street toward her buckboard with her head held high, I'm forced to admit this is about the silliest deal I ever brokered.

I stand at the window a few minutes, reflectin' on some of the other crazy deals I've brokered, which leads me to think of the deal I made for Gentry's first horse back in Rolla; which leads me to think about Gentry, and how I ain't seen nor heard from her since early this mornin'; which leads me to wonder what it'll take to get her talkin' to me again, and if so, will things ever be the same; and just as I'm thinkin' these woeful thoughts I catch sight of Penelope Way walkin' toward my office.

CHAPTER 17

THERE ARE TWO chairs in my office: one behind my desk, the other in front. It's been this way since I moved in eight months ago, but I never noticed how narrow my desk was till now, as Penelope takes a seat across from me. She's a couple inches taller than Gentry, and sits a little taller, so our eyes are nearly the same height. Lookin' into her face I have no idea what she's thinkin', or what she's about to say, which tells me she's better at hidin' her emotions than Gentry. One thing I love about Gentry is her sassy style. Penelope don't have that, but she does have a coltish man-ner that makes her spunkier and more spirited than the other Philadelphians. If those women were a herd of horses, Penelope would be the mustang at the edge, that don't quite fit in. You get the sense she's a handful: refined, like the others, but friskier, and harder to tame.

One thing that makes Penelope unique among women is the way she's content to look directly into my eyes for long periods of time without feelin' the need to say a word. She's doin' that now, in fact. Walked in, said nothin', took a seat, said nothin', stared into my eyes and *still* ain't said nothin'.

"How's Oliver?" I say.

"That depends."

"On what?"

"Whether or not he actually raped that woman. If he *did*, he's not suffering enough."

"I feel like he raped her."

"I gathered as much. What I don't understand is why you shot him."

"I had to distract the crowd."

She stares at me a moment, then nods. Then stares at me some more and says, "What makes you think he raped her?"

"I'd rather not say till after I get him in the jail cell."

"You don't trust me?"

"I don't trust his friends. Can I ask you a few questions?"

She fixes her eyes on mine and says, "You can ask me anything you want, Emmett, and I'll answer each...and *every* question...with *total* honesty."

That's no more than I'd expect of anyone, but the way she said it makes it sound like she's got somethin' else in mind.

I start things off, askin', "Does Oliver ever go out at night without you?"

"Virtually every night. Why?"

115

"You ever question him about it?"

"Of course. He says he's having a hard time adjusting to life in Dodge. In Philadelphia, he had a business to go to each day. Here, there's nothing for him to do."

"I thought he was buildin' houses."

"He is. As a laborer, not a contractor. So the work's not fulfilling, nor is there much money in it."

"Have you noticed any straw on his clothes lately?"

"You mean when he comes home after being out all night?"

"Yes."

She fiddles with the small coin purse hangin' over her shoulder. Then stares at me and says, "This sounds like a rather crucial question."

"It is indeed."

"I *have* noticed hay. However...."

"Yes?"

"I haven't noticed any scratches, scrapes, cuts, or bruises. Wouldn't I expect to?"

"Not necessarily."

"Correct me if I'm wrong, Sheriff, but—"

"What?"

She shakes her head. "I'm so sorry." She closes her eyes like she did somethin' wrong. "Please forgive me."

"For what?"

"I assumed a defensive tone. I called you Sheriff."

"I *am* the sheriff."

She touches my hand. "Dear Emmett." She sighs. "I trust you completely, and with all my heart."

"Well, I appreciate that. I trust you too."

"Thank you, Emmett. I've always felt we had a special type of trust between us."

"I think so too."

She smiles. "I can't tell you how happy I am to hear that!"

I shrug. It's not a major thing. I pretty much trust everyone till they give me a reason not to. And anyway, Penelope always struck me as bein' honest.

I ask, "Who are Oliver's closest friends?"

"Louis Hinkle and Anthony Evers, from Philadelphia, just as you'd expect."

"Has he mentioned anyone else?"

"Not to me. But I doubt there's anyone in New or Old Dodge he doesn't know by now."

I nod.

She licks her lips. "Is there anything else you'd like to ask me?" She pauses, lowers her voice to a whisper and says, "Because the answer will almost certainly be yes."

I take a minute to wonder what she thinks I might ask about Oliver that could get me a yes answer, and the only thing I come up with is to ask if he ever spoke about Amy. I hadn't thought to ask that, but it seems like a helluva good question.

"Has he ever spoken to you about Amy?"

She rolls her eyes. "Not that I recall."

"Tell me about the ring on his right hand."

"What about it?"

"How long has he had it?"

"Since boyhood."

"How often does he wear it?"

"Always."

"Have you ever seen one like it?"

"No. It belonged to his father."

"Is there anythin' special about the design? I mean, does it stand for somethin'?"

"I'm sure it does, but if he ever said, I've long since forgotten." She stares at me a moment, then widens her eyes. "Emmett? Isn't there something else you'd like to ask?"

She squeezes my hand lightly, and I suddenly realize her hand's been on mine this whole time! I wonder if it'd be rude to remove it. Then wonder if I really *want* to.

"Emmett?"

I look at her flawless face and say, "I have two more questions, but I'm hesitant to ask."

"Please ask them both," she says, givin' my hand another squeeze.

"The first is about Oliver."

She cocks her head, widens her eyes. "And the second?"

I take a quick breath and swallow before sayin', "My second question is about....us."

"Us?"

I nod.

CHAPTER 18

THE TEARS WELLIN' up in Penelope's eyes make 'em glisten the sparkly green color of the Kansas River in the summer sun.

"Ask your first question quickly, Emmett, so we can hurry to the second!"

"The first one's the easy one," I admit.

"Please hurry!"

"Very well. Has Oliver ever mentioned Miss Gilmore?"

She frowns. "The schoolteacher?"

I nod.

"Why do you ask?"

"I've been told somethin', but have no certain proof."

"Surely you don't think he raped Miss Gilmore too!"

"No."

"Then what?"

"I'd rather not say."

"Do you really trust me so little?"

"Again, it ain't you, Penelope."

She smiles. "You said my name."

"Huh?"

"I don't believe you've ever called me by my name before."

"I s'pect I must have."

"I think not. I'd remember."

"Well, I *should* have. It's a beautiful name."

She tilts her head. "Am I your only Penelope?"

"Only one *I* ever heard of."

She tosses her hair and beams with delight. "I'm so happy to hear that! Almost as happy as I'll be when you ask your second question. The one about us."

"You haven't answered about Miss Gilmore yet."

"Oh. Well yes, we've discussed Jean Gilmore on several occasions."

"In what manner?"

"I accused him of having an affair with her. Is it true?"

"What did he say?"

She laughs. "He denied it, of course. But a woman knows these things. It's true, isn't it?"

"It might be."

She sighs. "I suspected as much. It's one of the reasons we don't...ah...one of the *many* reasons we don't...."

Her face reddens.

I smile.

She smiles back and gives me a hopeful look. "Before you ask your question about us, can I be so bold as to ask if you dreamed about me last night?"

I make her look at me a few seconds before sayin', "That sounds like a rather crucial question." Teasin' her, since that's what she said to me a few minutes ago.

"Why Emmett!" she says. "You're witty!"

"You think?"

"Yes. But you haven't answered my question."

I bite the corner of my lip. Then say, "I probably shouldn't tell you this, but..."

The door suddenly bursts open. Penelope's hand flies back to her lap as fast as I ever drew a gun. I notice she don't turn around and I'm right glad of it, since she's blushin' fit to bust.

Except that she's left me to face the storm alone.

I sigh, and get to my feet like a guilty schoolboy, as....

CHAPTER 19

TWO PEOPLE ENTER my office: Penelope's friend, Amelia Evers, and Margaret Stallings, our Mayor. And Margaret's expression tells me she's been dragged here against her will. She says, "I'm sorry to interrupt, Emmett, but—"

Amelia rushes to Penelope's side. "Are you all right? Look at your face! My God, Penelope, what has he been *asking* you?"

She turns to me. "You should be ashamed of yourself!"

I *am* ashamed. But I'm also relieved, 'cause I was about to say some very improper things to Penelope that are far better left unsaid. I can't believe how quickly my emotions got out of control. I know it's wrong, but there's somethin' about Penelope that quickens my pulse, and draws me to her.

Even now, as I catch myself glancin' in her direction, I feel my heart pound. Like I say, I know it's wrong.

Every damn bit of it is wrong.

I'm havin' thoughts and dreams about Penelope that belong to Gentry.

But does Gentry even *want* 'em?

Margaret says, "Amelia, I've known Emmett for years. I can assure you he hasn't asked Penelope anything outside the boundaries of his investigation."

Amelia leans over and looks into Penelope's eyes. "Is that true?"

Penelope nods.

"Then what's wrong? Why are you so flushed?"

Penelope looks at me before sayin', "Wouldn't you be flushed to learn your husband's a rapist?"

Amelia frowns. "Oliver's nothing of the sort! What possible proof could anyone have that your husband—a civilized gentleman of the highest breeding and stature—would rape a...a degenerate woman of that ilk? A white squaw! A common...uh...."

She looks at my face and decides to stop right there, and that's a good thing, 'cause I clench my jaw and say, "Who the *hell* do you think you are? You have no fuckin' right to judge Amy Love. *No fuckin' right!* The things she's been through? The pain and sufferin' she's endured? I wouldn't give *ten* of you for one of her farts."

The women are stunned into silence. Even Penelope's shocked by my outburst. If Gentry were here she'd be just as appalled.

Or maybe not.

Margaret finally finds her voice. "Emmett...."

I wave her off and take a deep breath. "Ladies, I apologize. I'm not a...civilized gentleman of the highest breedin' and stature, or whatever the hell you said." I pause till Penelope looks up at me before addin', "And I never will be."

I turn my gaze to Margaret. "Why are you here?"

Amelia answers for her: "She's here on our behalf."

"Who's behalf are we talkin' about?"

"Penelope's. Oliver's. The people of Dodge."

Margaret says, "Is it true you shot Oliver in the foot before arresting him?"

I sigh. "Yup."

"Was he resisting arrest?"

I sigh again. "Nope."

"Two weeks ago you shot a reporter in the hand."

"He was interviewin' my daughter."

"You're wearing a badge, Emmett."

"You want it back?"

We look at each other a minute, then Margaret says, "I think we should all take a breath. No, Emmett, I don't want your badge. You're the best sheriff a town could ever have. In general."

"What's that mean?"

"It means you're a bit quick to shoot sometimes. You could have warned the reporter not to interview Scarlett. You could have arrested Oliver peacefully."

"I shot Oliver because May Gray got the crowd riled up to the point I felt someone was gonna get hurt."

"Someone *did* get hurt!" Amelia says. "Oliver got *shot!*"

"Oh, fiddle," I say, shakin' my head. "I grazed his smallest toe. He'll be fine in a day or two. Probably hurt himself worse by fallin' on the ground and rollin' around. As for the reporter, yeah, I could've warned him. But you know as well as me, he would've stayed in town and interviewed person after person and wrote whatever he wanted to make up. Next thing you know people would be comin' here by the hundreds to see if my daughter has healin' powers."

"But you shot a man."

"I shot the little flap of skin between his thumb and first finger. I guarantee you he ain't even wearin' a bandage by now."

Margaret says, "Amelia, I know Emmett's actions must appear severe to you, compared to how things are handled back East. But as you just heard, Emmett didn't fire his shots indiscriminately. He had a reason for his actions. And he's right about the flesh wounds. Neither Oliver nor the reporter were seriously injured."

"On the other hand," I say, "John Boone shot and killed a man in cold blood in front of a dozen witnesses and Amelia would have me set him free."

"That's a completely separate issue," Amelia says.

I look at Margaret. "Are we done here? 'Cause if so, I've got a prisoner to collect." I feel Penelope's eyes tryin' to get my attention, but I don't dare look at her. I've got an openin' here, and mean to take it.

Margaret says, "Will you do me one simple favor?"

"What?"

"Think before you shoot."

"I always do."

She sighs. "Carry on."

I wait for them to leave, but no one moves, so I say, "Want me to hold the door for you?"

Margaret says, "I think we should stay here till you put Oliver in a cell. As mayor, I'll want to hear the details surrounding the charges against him. I'll also want to review whatever evidence you've collected."

I nod. "That makes sense. What about them?"

Margaret says, "I'm certain Penelope will want to be with her husband as much as possible this evening, and since he'll be here soon, she might as well stay."

"And Amelia?"

"I'm Penelope's friend," Amelia says. "I shouldn't have allowed her to come here on her own in the first place."

"*Allowed* her? What are you, her ma?"

"Let's just say I'm the closest thing she has to a mother in this God-forsaken place."

"I reckon no one's forcin' you to stay."

"I suppose you'd be happier if we all packed up and left."

I want to say "If *you* left, absolutely!" But I don't. I've already said way too much already. I leave, go straight to the hotel, and ask Amy to meet me at my office in twenty minutes. Then I head to the *Spur* to formally arrest Oliver. With every step I take I wonder if Gentry will speak to me when we see each other.

And the answer is...yes.

In fact, she says....

CHAPTER 20

"HOW NICE OF you!"

"Huh?"

"You finally saw fit to show up."

"Well, I—"

"—after assuming I'd patch up your prisoner and sit with him for an hour while you interviewed his *wife!*"

"It had to be done, Gentry. And anyway, Margaret and Amelia were there. And before that, May Gray had to make a formal statement."

"Really? May Gray, the famous pecker-puller? I'll look forward to reading *her* statement!"

I frown, look at Oliver. "Get to your feet. You're under arrest."

Oliver rises, sayin', "I'm completely innocent of this charge. In the first place, I'd never have the slightest interest in fornicating with a woman of that class, a woman who looks like *that*. Why, I doubt there's a sadder creature or ug-lier face in the country, nor one who's been ridden by more Indians. Why, she's nothing but a common—"

"*Emmett!*" Gentry screams. "What the hell's the *matter* with you?"

Them are the only words Gentry managed to say before Oliver's body hit the ground.

I didn't shoot him, just punched his jaw.

To Gentry I say, "I'm sorry you think so poorly of me, but it's been a bad day. I love you, Gentry, but it's been a bad day."

She looks at me like she don't even know who I am. But then I see the slightest flicker in her eyes. I hear people in the saloon all around us, talkin', askin' questions, but all I care about is that tiny spark in Gentry's eyes. And then...she suddenly moves toward me, with outstretched arms.

"I love you too, Emmett!" she says. "And it's been a truly awful day for me, too."

Oliver's day goes from bad to worse as he regains con-sciousness just in time to feel Gentry step on his sore toe as she runs to me. He's screamin' in the background, but holdin' Gentry is all I can focus on at the moment. That, and the overwhelmin' sense of relief that I didn't say too much to Penelope a while ago. I see now I was inches away from destroyin' the best thing that ever happened to me.

We kiss, and every problem disappears.

"Thank God!" I say, knowin' in my heart I'll never have impure thoughts about Penelope, ever again. But just to make sure, I silently promise it to myself. And this time, it keeps.

For about ten minutes.

CHAPTER 21

AS I LEAD Oliver into my sheriff's office I notice the curious look Penelope's givin' me. Though I'm standin' in the doorway beside her husband who's not only hurt, but in the process of bein' jailed, it's *me* she's starin' at, as if she's wonderin' if somethin' has changed between us. I wonder if Margaret and Amelia can see how she's lookin' at me, compared to how she's lookin' at her husband.

When she looks at him at all, that is.

Not to mention it ain't Penelope, but Margaret who finally asks why Oliver's jaw's so swollen.

"Emmett punched my face," Oliver says. "Just hauled off and *punched* me!"

Amelia gets all puffed up and goes on a rant. Though Margaret and Oliver are hangin' on her every word, but Penelope ain't even *listenin'* to what her friend has to say. She's just starin' at me and—this is the really strange part—

somethin' sort of flashes in my eyes and I suddenly...okay, this ain't gonna make no sense at all, but...I can see her stark naked!

She's fully dressed, but it's almost as if I can see right through her clothes!

It only lasts a couple of seconds, but it's enough to make me halfway dizzy, which is somethin' I wouldn't expect for two reasons: first, I often see naked women at the *Spur* and it has no effect on me, and second, this vision of Penelope weren't real, 'cause I can see she's completely dressed.

I should explain the naked women comment. I don't spy on our whores. But they're a bawdy bunch that don't work a lick to hide their nakedness when I'm around. What I'm sayin', the site of a naked woman shouldn't cause me to be flustered, especially when it's only in my mind.

So why would Penelope's nakedness—if she *were* naked—send me to swoonin'?

Is it because she's a proper woman? Or is it because she's Penelope?

We stare at each other till Amelia finally talks herself out of words, at which point I tell Oliver to hand his ring over to Margaret. He does, and she studies it with great curiosity, but says nothin'. Then she, Amelia, and Penelope follow me and Oliver into the jail room, and watch me lock him up.

When John Boone sees the women he jumps to his feet and declares, "Merciful heavens! What do we have here? Three ladies, each of a different age, but all gorgeous to a fault. Please tell me you've entered the beauty contest!"

Amelia frowns, Penelope blushes, and Margaret...well, Margaret actually seems to be *sizing him up!* I recall my conversation with Boone yesterday and wonder if it's possible Margaret could be a former whore. If so, it must've been long ago and far away, as I've never heard talk of it. But it *would* explain her unusual tolerance for the gamblin', drinkin' and whorin' that thrives in Dodge City.

Margaret introduces herself, then the others. When she tells Boone that Penelope's married to Oliver, he says, "My dear, you've just broken my heart, as I was working up the courage to ask your permission to court you just now. Nevertheless, in the happy event your union leads to pregnancy, I hereby offer my services in delivering your offspring, free of charge."

"You're a dentist!" I say so quickly it takes a moment before I realize how angry my tone sounded. But Penelope noticed, and tries to hide a small, satisfied smile.

Boone says, "Oliver, you're the lucky fellow, aren't you? Apart from being arrested, I mean. What happened to your foot?"

"The sheriff shot me."

"And did he strike your cheek as well?"

"First, he shot me in the foot. Then his wife sewed it up. Then she stomped on it, and somewhere along the way he punched my face."

Oliver frowns and looks at me. "Could this possibly be true? If so, I think a case can be brought against Sheriff Love for excessive use of force, and I might be persuaded to add it to his murder charge."

"What murder charge?" I ask.

He ignores me and asks Oliver if he's engaged the services of an attorney yet.

I say, "We don't have any attorneys in Dodge. And if you ask me, we're better off for it."

"I didn't ask you. But since you brought it up, I'll have to vehemently disagree, and wonder if you're truly telling me that men go to trial in this city without the benefit of legal representation."

"We generally leave it up to the circuit judge to sort out who's innocent or guilty."

"And how has that worked out for the accused?"

"The majority of 'em tend to be hanged."

"Unacceptable. Oliver, I'll take your case. We can prepare it tonight from our jail cells."

"That's the first good news I've had today," Oliver says. "Did you hear that, Penelope?"

She did, but she don't comment. So I say, "You might want to rethink havin' a killer dentist representin' you in front of a judge."

Oliver says, "Mr. Boone, pardon my asking, but do you have legal experience?"

Boone laughs. "Do the words Harvard College mean anything to you?"

"Of course! It's the single most prestigious university in the country."

"Country?" Boone sniffs.

"World?" Oliver says.

"Thank you," Boone says. He looks at me. "Not many men can say they have a law degree from Harvard."

"I agree. Can *you?*"

"Can I what?"

"Say you have a law degree from Harvard."

"You mean because I'm a dentist?"

"Well *are* you?"

"Perhaps I should clarify."

"That'd be a welcome twist."

"Any man in possession of a pair of pliers can claim to be a dentist," Boone says. "But do you know how many men across this vast nation have an actual *degree* in dentisty?"

"Nope."

He puffs up in a bossy sort of way that reminds me of Amelia and says, "There are but three dental colleges in the United States. The first and best was founded in 1840 by an act of the Maryland General Assembly."

"So?"

"It's first graduating class had two members. Do you understand the magnitude of that statement?"

"No."

"It means twenty-six years ago there were only two certified dentists in the entire United States."

"And now?"

"Now what?"

"How many are there?"

He shrugs. "How would *I* know? Only a *charlatan* would attempt a guess." He tips his hat to Penelope and says, "Please forgive my strong use of language."

She looks at him curiously, but says nothin'.

Boone says, "I can only tell you how many students mastered the rigorous curriculum of the Baltimore College of Dental Surgery the year I graduated: fifteen."

"And were you one of 'em?"

He shows me a look of exasperation. "What did I just tell you?"

"I ain't sure."

Boone smugly turns to Oliver and says, "Let's discuss my fee."

Oliver says, "That's going to be a problem, as Penelope and I are currently receiving but a small stipend from her father. Apart from that, the amount I generate as a day laborer is quite meager."

"What's your occupation?"

"In Philadelphia I was a contractor. Here, I'm a carpenter, and day-laborer."

"Excellent! You can build my new office. In return, I'll keep you out of jail."

"What about materials?"

"I'll get someone else to contribute everything you'll need to build a first-rate office."

"How?"

"Truth be told, I expect to have the deal struck in the next twenty minutes."

Oliver says, "I don't see how that's possible, but you've got yourself a client!"

I say, "Don't celebrate your victory too quickly, Oliver. Mr. Boone might not be around to represent you. He's waitin' on a trial date for murder."

"Not to worry," Boone says. "There'll be no murder charge."

"How you figure that?"

"May Gray informed me earlier today that Eli Shed didn't die from a gunshot. According to her, his head blew up. Now unless you've got some sort of magic bullet theory, my shot couldn't have killed him. But under whose care was Mr. Shed when his head burst into flames? Yours! Did you set his head on fire or blow it off his shoulders with a shotgun?"

"Neither."

"So you say. But I plan to file charges against you for murdering him."

"That's ridiculous."

"Is it? I'm told your wife and daughter were witnesses to his death. The way I see it, you have two choices: I can personally file the charges and oppose you in court, or I can have someone else file them and you can hire me to represent you. If I'm arguing *against* you, you'll surely hang. But if I'm representing you, I can guarantee you'll be found innocent, assuming the case ever gets to court, which I seriously doubt. My fee for representing you will be no more nor less than a free and clear deed to your best remaining commercial lot on Main Street."

"Maybe we should cross that bridge when we come to it."

He waves his hand. "It's your funeral. But remember, they can't try me for murder if the man's head blew up."

"You can still be tried for shootin' him."

"I won't be found guilty. The man was a pervert and a murderer, and the town is safer without him. You said so yourself."

"Maybe so, but you didn't know that before you shot him."

"How can you possibly say that?"

"What do you mean?"

"How do you know I wasn't walking past Eli's house at the precise moment he shot his wife? Who can say I didn't rush in after seeing him leave? Who can say I didn't hear her dying words, her grief-stricken tale of woe?"

"*What* tale of woe?"

"That their fight—far from being about money—was due to her discovering his predilection for school children!"

"His what?"

"Who's to say she didn't look up at me from her death-bed with heartsick eyes and implore me to march into that saloon and shoot her husband, Eli Shed, before he had the opportunity to despoil the innocence of several children of Dodge?"

I frown. "If that's your story you better have an explanation as to why you consorted with a number of hallway whores before confrontin' him."

"That's an excellent observation, Sir, and one I'll be prepared to answer at the proper time."

"The judge might also wonder why you didn't mention any of this at the time of your arrest."

"No one asked me."

"*I* asked you."

"Did you? I must not have heard. There was quite a bit of commotion, after all."

"I like your style," Oliver says.

Boone smiles. "Just wait till you see how quickly I get *your* case dismissed. What's the charge?"

"Rape."

"*Really? Why, that's wonderful!*"

"It *is? Why?*"

"There are so many possible defenses!"

"Like what?"

"She's lying. It was consensual. She led you on and had it coming. You were set up. It's a case of mistaken identity. Take your pick, but the bottom line is, where's her proof?"

I say, "This is gettin' ridiculous. Penelope, if you'd like to visit with Oliver alone for a few minutes, I'll take Boone outside for a walk."

She says, "I'll speak to Oliver after I hear the evidence you have against him. I assume it has something to do with his ring."

"What ring?" Boone says, as we hear a knock in the next room, at my office door.

I tell Oliver to sit on his cot and put the blanket over his head and keep it there till I tell him different. Then I go to the front door, let Amy in, and escort her into the jail room.

Amelia says, "What's *she* doing here?"

"I'd like you all to look at Amy's forehead, right here," I say, pointin' to the mark I noticed earlier, at the stable. "Margaret, hold Oliver's ring next to it."

She does.

"I'd call that a perfect match, wouldn't you?"

Penelope would, and she nods.

Margaret would, and *she* nods.

John Boone says, "That mark could have been made by anything of a similar design, not that it matters, since a mark on the head isn't proof of rape."

"It shows he hit her," I say.

"It shows nothing of the sort. But even if he did, it's not proof of a sexual assault."

I notice Amy studyin' the ring. She says, "I have that same imprint on several parts of my body."

Margaret says, "If I have the others turn away, will you show me?"

"I'm not proud of what you'll see."

"What do you mean?"

"My body's been spoiled far worse than my face and head."

"I'd still like to see. It's evidence."

Before any of us can turn around, Amy removes her shirt.

Penelope cries out.

Amelia shudders.

I wince, and bite my lip.

Margaret seems to only notice the ring marks, and counts five: three on her ribs, one on her shoulder, one on her stomach.

"I notice they're all on the same side of your body," Margaret says.

I say, "It's what you'd expect to see if a man was facing her, hitting her with his right fist. I'm sure you noticed Oliver wears his ring on his right hand."

Amelia says, "Put your blouse back on, Mrs. Love. You're making us terribly uncomfortable. You're no longer among savages, and your body's a disgrace to womanhood."

We're all shocked by her harsh words, but it's Penelope who says, "That's *quite enough*, Amelia!" She stares at her in disbelief. "What's *happened* to you? Where's your *heart*?"

The tears streamin' down Penelope's face don't surprise me. She's always seemed kind-hearted to me. But what *does* surprise me is how she rushes over to Amy and hugs her close and helps her back into her shirt and says, "I'm so sorry, Amy. Not just for what my husband did, but for what I've done. I've shunned you." She kisses Amy's cheek. "I should have reached out to you in a friendly manner and welcomed you to the community." She shakes her head sorrowfully and says, "I'm a better person than what I've shown. I hope you'll give me a chance to prove it."

"What do you mean?" Amy says.

"I'd like to be your friend."

Amy don't quite know what to say, but what comes out of her mouth is the strange comment, "I'm staying at the hotel."

Penelope nods. "When we're finished here, we'll go to my home. I'll feed you a proper meal and get you outfitted with clean clothes. Then I'll walk you back to the hotel. Tomorrow morning, I'll pay you a visit."

Amelia huffs, "That's all well and good, Penelope, but you know what strikes *me* as odd? It appears *I'm* more interested in defending your husband than *you* are. Meanwhile, you're befriending his *accuser*."

"I can see why you'd say that, Amelia. Then again, you're not the one who's living with Oliver, or cleaning the stable hay from his clothes every night."

Amelia frowns. "Sheriff, I'll admit Oliver's ring is similar to the marks on Amy's body. But I'm sure if I went to the river I could find a rock to match that same mark within minutes."

Boone adds, "Well said, Amelia. But the ring mark means nothing, as it will be healed long before Oliver's court date. And even if the mark was made by Oliver's ring there's no proof he was wearing it at the time of the assault. And if he was, and if he hit her repeatedly for whatever reason—including defending himself from an attempted robbery—it doesn't prove he raped her."

I look at Amy. "How many men raped you each night?"

"Three."

"Would you be able to recognize any of them?"

"I'd be able to recognize *all* of them."

That shuts Boone up.

I say, "How about we take a look at the man under the blanket?"

CHAPTER 22

"I DON'T NEED to *see* him," Amy says. "I'll know him from his voice."

Boone says, "His *voice?* Are you saying you can't identify the men who raped you by any means other than your sense of hearing?"

"It was dark," Amy says, looking at me for help.

I say, "It's a well-known fact Masikotas teach their women and children how to distinguish voices in the dark. They're well-skilled at it."

"That's awfully convenient," Boone says, "or it *would* be, if Amy were an Indian. But in any case, I can assure you no court of law will accept verbal identification."

"That ain't true," I say. "I heard a blind man testify he recognized his neighbor's voice as the man who stabbed him, and the judge accepted it."

"There's a far cry between recognizing a neighbor's voice and being able to identify the voices of three strangers who allegedly raped her."

"I don't see why."

"If Mrs. Love picks out my client based on the sound of his voice I'll simply explain that the men who raped her—if anyone actually *did*—were disguising their voices."

"But if she *recognizes* the voices..."

"Perhaps the rapists are gifted vocal impersonators. How would you feel if I could mimic your voice perfectly, and went around raping women, and talking to them in order to shift the blame to you?"

"You think the judge is gonna believe three men in one town can imitate three other men?"

"He doesn't have to believe it, but he'll have to accept it as a possibility."

"I reckon if Oliver dressed up like a horse you'd claim a horse committed the crime."

"Now you're on the right track, Sheriff. Criminals disguise their looks all the time. But here's a better example: you know how young men's voices change when they come of age? If the courts were allowed to identify criminals based on the sound of their voices, every eleven-year-old boy in the country could commit a crime and get away with it the day his voice turns deeper."

The women and I look at each other.

Boone says, "My offer to represent you at your murder trial is still on the table, but it won't be for long."

I sigh. "Well, I didn't murder Eli, but since you've got more answers than a fortune teller, I reckon I'd better take you up on it, if I'm charged."

"You know what you should do?"

"What's that?"

"Put me on retainer."

"What's that mean?"

"It means I'll always be your attorney, and represent you in any court case."

"Forever?"

"As long as I'm on retainer."

"What if someone else has you on retainer, and they sue me?"

"My loyalties are to my clients in the order they sign up. If you say yes, you'll be my first. I'll represent you against everyone, except myself. And I'll represent my second client against everyone except you and me."

"What would *that* cost?"

"I'm not a greedy man. In addition to the commercial lot, which is my fee for representing you at your murder trial, I'll only ask for the materials needed to build my office."

Oliver shouts, "Wait! *I* want to be your first client!"

Amy shouts, "That voice! He's one of the men who raped me!"

Oliver: "*Shit!*"

Penelope: "You *bastard!*"

Margaret says, "Mr. Boone, I'd like to put you on retainer myself."

I say, "Seems to me you could get money from everyone in town by threatenin' to sue 'em."

"That's right, Sheriff," he says, "and they'd be crazy not to pay. So how about it? You want to be my first client, or should I give that opportunity to Oliver or Margaret?"

I take my hat off again, run my fingers through my hair and say, "In the space of thirty minutes—while behind bars—you've negotiated a free lot, building materials for an office, and the labor it takes to build it."

"That's right. And all three of us got a good deal....So, are you in or out?"

I shrug. "I reckon I'm in."

I ain't signin' up 'cause I fear the man, but because I'm worried for Scarlett. If Boone accuses me of murder, Scarlett might tell the judge she's the one who made Eli's head blow up, and I can't think of anythin' good that'll come from *that* revelation.

"Excellent," Boone says. "You've made a wise choice. If you'll bring me some paper, pen, and ink, I'll memorialize the details in a contract."

I bring him what he asked for, and he writes up a short agreement. After we sign it I say, "Now that you're my attorney, I want you to sue Oliver's friends for rapin' Amy."

He looks puzzled. "How have *you* been harmed by her rape?"

"She's my wife."

"I'll need more."

"Amy's so upset over bein' raped she can't perform her wifely duties, so I'm gonna have to divorce her. And since I've lost my marriage 'cause of what these men did to her...."

Boone's face brightens. "You can sue them for aliena-tion of affection and destruction of marriage. We'll file the suit the moment they're found guilty of rape."

Oliver says, "Wait. What about me?"

Boone says, "Sheriff, if Oliver names the other two and testifies against them, would you be willing to work out a settlement with him apart from the others?"

"I'll settle for his testimony against the others and his immediate labor in buildin' Amy's house."

Oliver says, "That's insane!"

Boone says, "As your lawyer, I recommend you accept the Sheriff's proposal. You won't be charged, you won't be hanged, and all you have to do is testify against the others, and build an office, and house."

"A house and an office," I say. "In that order."

Boone looks at Amy, then nods. "Very well. And to show my sympathy for her plight, I'll represent Amy for free in the criminal case."

I say, "Thank you. Can you go ahead and write up di-vorce papers for me and Amy?"

"Certainly."

Penelope says, "That's one down and one to go!"

Everyone pauses to stare at her. She blushes and says, "Please forgive me, Emmett. I have no idea why I said that."

Boone says, "In light of Oliver's plans to turn state's witness against the men who raped Amy, I'll ask for his im-mediate release."

"Normally I'd release him," I say, "but I think his life might be in danger."

Boone looks at me and smiles. "I may have misjudged you, Sheriff." He turns to Oliver and says, "The sheriff makes a good point. You'll want to stay here till the others are arrested. In the meantime, I'll need a written statement from you, explaining who the men are, and how you know they raped Amy."

I notice Amelia starin' holes through Oliver. He sees it too, and says, "I can't testify against my friends."

"Why not?" Boone says.

Penelope says, "Because Amelia's husband, Anthony, is one of the men." She turns to her friend. "That's why you've been acting so dreadfully from the moment Oliver was arrested."

"I'm not going to discuss this with you," Amelia says.

I figured from the start the other Philadelphians were involved, and it's been botherin' me for hours. On the one hand, Amy deserves her day in court. On the other, these men were the first Philadelphians to settle in Dodge, and dozens more are already here or on their way due to their efforts. If Oliver won't testify against his friends, it'll be hard to convict them when the judge finds out about Amy's history with the Indians, and hears she didn't fight back, and learns she can't recognize the men apart from their voices and scents. And of course, her wounds—includin' the ring mark—will be healed long before a circuit judge shows up. Obviously she's loaded with permanent scars, but she's had those since the day she entered Dodge, so them wounds can't be blamed on the Philadelphians.

Bottom line, they're gonna get away with it. Unless....

I look at my former wife. "Can you and me go outside and talk a minute?"

She nods, and follows me outside, and I say, "I know gettin' raped by these three men was a terrible thing."

She looks at me. "Are you suggesting we let them get away with it?"

"Not at all. But you've been raped by hundreds of men...*and* these three. In my opinion they *all* deserve to be hanged, but I ain't sure the judge'll side with you, since you already admitted you didn't fight back and can't identify their faces."

"What should I do?"

"I can't say, but I'll give you three choices: first, you can sue all three of 'em for rape. If they're found guilty, they'll hang. But if the judge lets 'em walk, you'll get nothin'. Either way, I s'pect at least half the town will hold a grudge against you, and that ain't a good thing. Second, we can both sue 'em and scare 'em into a cash settlement. Maybe we could get 'em to pay you a fee every month for the rest of your life."

"What's the third choice?"

"I can kill 'em for you."

She thinks a moment, then says, "How much do you think they'll pay?"

CHAPTER 23

Two Days Later...

ME AND GENTRY are back to normal. What I mean is, we're doin' all them romantic things we used to do before Scarlett entered our lives. That ain't to say we don't love Scarlett dearly. We do. But havin' her in the house weren't the best way to keep the fires of romance burnin'. Last time me and Gentry had the opportunity to share some romantic time together Scarlett knocked on the door and said, "Are you through fornicating yet?"

We weren't, but we stopped.

Then she said, "Does it always take six minutes to fornicate?"

Right now Gentry and me are in the rollin' field north of Dodge with Rudy, our bear, and it strikes me I can't hardly remember the last time we brought him here to dig tubers. We thought he'd want to play tag like the old days, but he smells tubers, and I ain't met the bear yet that'd put tag ahead of tubers.

"If he's eatin', we're eatin'," I say.

I can tell Gentry's disappointed, but I ain't. Last time I played tag with Rudy he smacked me so hard my shoulder separated. Somethin' about me bein' in pain obviously tickled his funny bone, 'cause the more I winced the harder he laughed.

As I spread our picnic lunch on our blanket, Gentry says, "I'm surprised Oliver refused to press charges against you."

Gentry don't know about the deal we worked with Oliver and the others that raped Amy. Two nights ago Amelia brought 'em to my office quietly, in the dead of night, and they each agreed to pay Amy twenty dollars a month for the rest of her life. In return, all seven of us who were in my office that night: Amelia, Amy, Penelope, Oliver, me, Margaret, and John Boone—agreed not to tell anyone what really happened. The next mornin' I released Oliver, and publicly apologized for shootin' him, and said his arrest had been based on a misunderstandin'. Margaret softened it by sayin' I had acted reasonably based on the information I had at the time. Surprisin'ly, no one asked for details after Oliver made a public announcement sayin' he had no intention of pressin' charges against me, as it had been an honest mistake. Before makin' the agreement, I told all three men if I ever find out they've raped another woman, they'd better hide two ways: fast and long.

"What really happened, Emmett?" Gentry asks.

"I can't tell you. I entered into an agreement, and it wouldn't be right to say."

"I'm your wife."

"You are. And I love you."

She sighs. "I'd like to think we had no secrets."

"I'd like that, too. But this ain't a secret that involves you and me."

"Who else knows?"

"I can't say."

"Can't or won't?"

"Won't."

She frowns.

It don't set well with me not to personally punish these men beyond the financial payments they'll have to make, but I know the circuit judge would never have convicted 'em, so it was either kill 'em or make 'em pay the victim. Thankfully, Amy made that decision for me. Two of the wives—Amelia and Penelope—know the details, 'cause they were there. But their best friend, Winnifred Hinkle, don't know her husband, Louis, is a rapist, which is why she's havin' a hard time understandin' why Penelope and Amelia ain't speakin' to Louis or their own husbands.

It ain't like the three Philadelphians won't suffer. It'll stick in their craw every month when I come around to collect their payments, so they'll never be allowed to forget what they done. Also, their three families will never be the same. Their lifetime of close friendship is over. It helps me knowin' Amy will be better off with a house and a lifetime income than she'd be if they went to trial, 'cause even if they were found guilty and sentenced to hangin', she'd get no benefit from it.

These are the thoughts I'm thinkin' as I notice Shrug boundin' down the far hill, headin' toward us at a fast clip.

CHAPTER 24

ME AND SHRUG don't talk about his trip till he's had a chance to share our meal and play with Rudy. When that's done, he hands me a piece of paper I can't read. I mean, I can recognize some of the words, I just can't figure out what they mean. I look at Shrug.

"Do you understand this?"

He shakes his head.

I hand it to Gentry, and she gives up too.

I put the paper in my saddlebag and leave it be till we end the picnic and walk back to town. I let Shrug and Gentry take Rudy back to the saloon, and I bring the paper to John Boone.

He reads it and laughs.

I ask him what's so funny.

He says, "It's a court order from the Wichita County Judge that involves my future."

"So?"

"You trust me to tell you what it says?"

"I'm willin' to hear what you've got to say about it."

"How would you know if I'm telling you the truth?"

"I wouldn't. But you're my attorney."

"I'm also your prisoner."

"I'm willin' to listen."

"It's a Writ of Habeas Corpus."

"What's that mean?"

Boone smiles. "It's Latin."

"What's that?"

"The language of laws."

"What's it mean?"

"It means Kansas State Judge Earl Lobotomy has weighed the facts of the case and decided it doesn't merit a trial. It orders the immediate release of the prisoner. That's me, by the way."

"You were right the first time," I say. "I don't believe you."

"Maybe you should ask someone else to read it to you."

"I reckon I will."

I take the paper to Miss Gilmore's house, and hear some noises comin' from within', but she don't come to the door, which makes me believe Penelope's husband might be inside. I go to the side of the house where her bedroom's located and bang on the wall. "Miss Gilmore, do you speak Latin?"

She don't answer.

I call out, "I've got a piece of paper from the court in Wichita that involves my prisoner, John Boone. A lot of the words are in Latin, and I don't know what they're orderin' me to do."

I listen to the silence. Then say, "A man's freedom's at stake. I'm gonna keep knockin' on your wall till you answer me."

I hear some movement inside. Then, with a very unfriendly tone, she says, "Come to the front door."

I do, but she don't invite me in. I hand her the paper and she says, "I can translate the words, but they don't make sense to me."

"Why not?"

"They refer to legal situations."

"What's the first part mean?"

"Writ of Habeas Corpus?"

"Yeah."

"It literally means, produce the body."

"What body?"

"I can only assume they're referring to the deceased."

"Eli *Shed*?"

"Is there any *other* body?"

"Eli's been taken to Fort Dodge to be buried. I s'pect he's six feet under."

"I fail to see how that's any of my concern."

"You think they expect me to dig up Eli's body and drag it to Wichita?"

"Yes."

"Well that don't make no sense."

"Try to remember you're dealing with the government. Are we done here, Sheriff?"

"You and me?"

"Yes."

"No."

She sighs. "What else?"

"Does it say anything in there about releasing my prisoner?"

She pauses a moment, then says, "You need to deliver the victim's body to the court issuing the order. Once there, he'll stand trial."

"Stand *trial*? He's a *corpse*!"

"I'm interpreting as best I can, but I won't be held responsible. I already told you I have no legal training."

"You know anyone who's smart enough to understand it?"

"Maybe you should ask Scarlett."

I frown.

"Anything else?" she asks, with great irritation.

"Yeah," I say. "Your dress is inside out."

I head back to the jail and say, "What does habeas corpus mean?"

"Literally?" Boone says.

"Yes."

"Produce the body."

"Are you tellin' me the state court in Wichita expects me to dig up Eli Shed's body and bring it to them?"

He gives me a strange look. Then says, "Who told you that?"

"Miss Gilmore."

"And she is?"

"The school marm."

He nods. "She's quite bright. Haven't met her, though I'd love to. Would you say she's large-chested?"

I frown.

He says, "I'll be glad to help you exhume Mr. Shed's body and accompany you to Wichita."

"You ain't afraid to go to the Wichita court?"

"Why would I be afraid? They've ordered you to set me free."

I shake my head. "So that's what I'm supposed to do? Dig up the body and take it to Wichita?"

"You think Miss Gilmore and I could both be leading you astray?"

"I don't know what to think."

"Can I make a suggestion?"

"Go ahead."

"Release me on my own recognizance."

"What's that mean?"

"It means I promise to remain in town and stay out of trouble. That way you won't have to worry about my well-being while you're gone."

"My friend Shrug will watch over you."

"So you're going?"

I study the paper a minute, then say, "I reckon I have to. Can I ask you a question?"

"Of course."

"Why'd you kill Eli?"

"Confidentially?"

I nod.

"Have you ever heard of Thomas Ewing, Jr.?"

"Not as I recall."

"He was the first Chief Justice of the State of Kansas."

"So?"

"When the war broke out, he became a Brigadier General, and had all the women who helped Confederate raiders rounded up and put in jail. One day the jail's roof collapsed and five women died. It's the main reason Quantrill attacked Lawrence, Kansas in August, 1863."

"I *knew* Quantrill! He attacked the soldiers that held me prisoner. It's thanks to him I survived the war."

"Then you of all people should understand."

"Understand what?"

"Why I killed Eli Shed."

"I ain't sure what you're tryin' to say."

"Who do you think ran the jail where those poor women were crushed to death?"

"Eli Shed?"

"And who do you think abused those women every single day and night?"

"Eli Shed?"

Boone lies down on his cot, closes his eyes. I say, "Was Eli Shed in charge of the jail or not?"

Boone says nothin'.

It strikes me the whole story he just told me might never have happened. Or if it did, it might not have involved Eli at all.

But I have to admit, it's a helluva story.

I say, "I reckon I'll see you when I see you."

He opens his eyes. "Where are you going?"

"To rent a buckboard wagon."

He laughs. "Good luck with that."

"What do you mean?"

"Didn't you burn up the last one?"

"I reckon the Philadelphians will rent me one of theirs."

He nods. "I expect you're right. But as your attorney I feel compelled to say something."

"What's that?"

"If they refuse you the buckboard, don't shoot them."

"They won't refuse."

CHAPTER 25

THE SOLDIERS AT Fort Dodge can't remember which grave they put Eli Shed in until I produce a twenty-dollar gold piece, at which point they have a fistfight to see who gets to dig him up. I watch the winner pull four bodies out of a recently-dug grave before he locates Eli.

Before lettin' him load the rottin', stinkin' body onto Louis Hinkle's buckboard wagon, I remove my saddlebag and the carpetbag I borrowed from Gentry, and secure them to the outside wall of the wagon. When I nod my head, the soldier drops Eli into the wagon hard enough to send a wave of dirt, blood, and guts two feet in every direction. I can only wonder how horrified Hinkle's wife would be to see Eli's bowels and body fluids leakin' into the bottom of her family's fine buckboard, saturatin' the wood, and drippin' through the floorboards onto the ground below. I didn't tell

Louis what I planned to *do* with his buckboard, just what I'd do to *him* if he didn't rent it to me.

Eli's flesh is comin' off his body in sheets, and the stench oozin' out from under it is as putrid and foul as a buffalo hunter's ass.

I sigh.

Only thing I hate worse than wagon travel is stage coach travel. The bouncin' around on hard seats messes up my neck, shoulders, and lower back somethin' awful. If I don't stop every hour durin' the journey, I'll be laid up for days.

I look at Eli's corpse and curse, knowin' I'm facin' a god-awful two to three-day wagon ride to Wichita. I briefly think about tyin' a rope around his body and draggin' him behind Hinkle's horse. If I did that I could get to Wichita in half the time, but Eli's corpse would never survive the trip. When the soldier was diggin' up the body his shovel blade cut into Eli's neck and shoulder such that what's left of his burned-up head and one of his arms ain't likely to stay attached to his torso too long after the buckboard starts bouncin' over the rugged trail.

Hinkle's horse don't like the smell any more'n I do. His nostrils are flarin' somethin' fierce, and he's tryin' to rear up and break the wagon poles loose from the tug loops.

I ease him best I can and say, "Ain't nothin' to do but get it done."

I can't bring myself to imagine how sorry this trip's gonna be and how many days it'll take to get the stink out of my nose and clothes when it's finally over. I take a minute to think about my sweet Gentry, who'll be home alone the whole week we'd hoped to spend some special romantic time together, and wonder why the hell I ever decided to be a lawman.

There's only one savin' grace about this whole Wichita business: before I left town this mornin', Margaret caught up with me and said the women asked her to hold the beauty contest this comin' Sunday instead of whatever day they originally planned. I told her I probably wouldn't be back till Monday, and she agreed to judge it for me. I was so relieved I almost started lookin' forward to the trip ahead.

Till now.

I climb on the wagon seat, slap the horse's fanny with the reins, and get about two feet before the bouncin' commences. The wheels are made of wood, and the ground is hard, so every rock, clod, and wagon rut jolts my body and makes the wagon pitch and bounce. And every time it does, Eli's body thumps and rattles like a load of lumber planks, causin' his death smells to waft up and make me gag. This happens eight times the first minute, and I know it's only gonna get worse in the hours and days ahead, since part of the land I'll be crossin' ain't been cleared to the extent of where I'm at right now, which is the Santa Fe Trail.

As I travel mile after weary mile I marvel at the sheer number of Easterners travelin' west. The land here's flat as a corn cake, and the clearness of the day allows me to see about three miles in every direction. Out of all that area I appear to be the only one headin' east. The trail I'm followin' is about four miles wide and I'm slap in the middle of it, which gives 20 prairie schooners per hour the opportunity to pass me close enough to holler things like, "Givin' up?" and "You're headin' the wrong way!" and "Have you seen any Indians?" and "How far to the Rockies?" and "Good God! Is that a dead *body* in your wagon?"

I think about how all these people gave up their homes and lives to find happiness in Colorado or California, and how most of 'em ain't prepared for how far them places are from here, and how they're gonna wind up somewhere on the Kansas plains for at least a year or two, and if they do make it to Colorado I reckon they're likely to be deeply disappointed when they learn how sparse the towns are, provision-wise, and how hard the life's gonna be. I'm sure these folks have lived through hard times and harsh winters, but them that end up in the Rockies or on the Kansas plains ain't got a clue what they're in for. I doubt there's anythin' can prepare an Easterner for the dreariness and loneliness of livin' in almost total isolation, and havin' to survive off what little the land affords.

It sounds romantic when you're back East, thinkin' about movin' away from civilization, livin' in a nice little cottage in the Kansas woods, surrounded by your wife and kids, havin' a jackrabbit dinner in front of a roarin' fire. But what the "Go West!" folks don't tell you is there ain't no woods in Kansas, nor any wood at *all*, for that matter. In fact, wood is so sparse in Kansas you're not likely to find enough to build a small *fire*, let alone a house! You want a wooden house in Kansas, you'll have to stop in a larger town along the way and buy several wagon loads of lumber and hope the owner of the lumberyard's honest enough to actually deliver it to wherever you tell him. And even if he's honest it don't mean his wagons won't be stolen by some of the hundreds of outlaws who make a livin' stealin' wagons and lumber meant for others. And if you *do* order lumber, be sure to pay special attention to that part of the contract that says delivery times may vary, 'cause they sure as shit will! I ain't met the man yet who got his lumber when he thought he would, and often it don't arrive the same *year!*

Nope, if you're bound for Kansas, you won't be livin' in no wooden house the first year unless you settle in a town like Dodge and buy a house from someone who's already built one. If you're intention is to live on the plains you'll be lucky to survive the winter, and if you do, it'll be in a sod hut. And as I say, you won't be burnin' wood for your fire, you'll be burnin' horse or cow patties, if you can find 'em, and *people* patties if you can't.

They don't tell you about people patties back East when they're charmin' you into movin' to the Kansas plains.

People patties are made by the members of your family, who shit in the same spot till a large mound is formed. Then you or your wife will mix some grass into that stack of shit and mold it into a brick or block and wait till it dries out. Meanwhile, your family will shit in a new spot. When the shit bricks are dry, you'll bring 'em into your sod house and burn 'em in your fireplace, assumin' you were able to collect enough river rocks to build a fireplace. If not, you'll attempt to build a fire on the rocks you *were* able to find, and hope the smoke goes up and out of the hole you made in the sod roof for that purpose. But even with a rock fireplace you'll find that only half the smoke travels up and out, and the rest fans out into the hut. This is especially true when the wind's blowin' severe, which it tends to do about 90% of the time. In fact, most of the time the wind blows so hard you won't be able to keep your shit fire lit long enough to cook a meal. When you *can* keep it lit you'll be surprised how little the shit bricks smell if you dried 'em long enough, and how bad they smell if you didn't. Either way, you'll plan your day around your cookin' 'cause you can't be inside very long with all that smoke, 'cause it'll tear your lungs up. So you start tryin' to build your fire around three in the afternoon, and when the smoke starts billowin' inside you'll find things to do outside while your meal warms up enough to choke it down around four o'clock. You'll put the fire out and eat that meal outside and hope the inside smoke clears enough by night time so you can go back inside, where you have a better chance against the nocturnal critters. In the colder months you'll avoid buildin' that fire till you can't stand it no more, and the only way you'll be able to handle the smoke is to poke holes in the sod walls near your face. You won't sleep too well in the winter, worryin' about critters comin' in through them holes in the wall, and 'cause you'll be keepin' an eye on your wife and kids to make sure they don't roll over in their sleep to where their noses and mouths are facin' the fire instead of the holes, in which case they could die from inhalin' too much smoke.

As for shootin' jackrabbits for dinner? Good luck with that, unless you thought to bring a shotgun, which most Easterners don't. What they tend to bring is rifles, and there ain't many Easterners I've met can shoot a jackrabbit with a rifle. Prairie dogs are easier to hit, but not cleanly, which means you'll use more ammunition than you think. Who on the trail ain't heard five shots only to come up on an Easterner skinnin' a single prairie dog? And yes, it's meat, but it's greasy, and don't taste nearly as good as rabbits. Still, like I say, it's meat, and you'll gladly take it if you can get it. But if you're livin' on the Kansas plains I s'pect most of your meals will consist of grain cakes, if you've got grain, and grass soup if you don't. Assumin' you've got water.

Occasionally you'll see an Easterner with a cow. You know what me and Shrug call that? A temporary luxury. Them who bring a cow will have milk to drink and cow patties to burn till the wolves, Indians, or outlaws take it from you. And they *will* take it from you, bein' that milk cows are the most highly-prized possessions a man can have. An Indian or outlaw may or may not try to steal your wife or kids, but they'll always steal your cow. There ain't an Indian in the west who wouldn't put his life on the line to take your milk cow. You think you and your wife and kids can protect that cow? Why, even the soldiers at Fort Dodge couldn't keep their cows from gettin' stole, and that's 200 soldiers!

Speakin' of soldiers, that's a sad bunch who *really* have it bad. Fort Dodge is the sorriest place you'll find in the West. First off, it ain't much of a fort, since there ain't a scrap of wood on the entire property. This is more than 200 men livin' in 70 dugouts they hand-carved out of the north bank of the Arkansas River, ten feet by twelve feet, and seven feet deep. Each dugout sleeps four cramped soldiers and has an openin' that faces the river, and a hole in the sod roof to let light and air in. They don't have room for fireplaces in their huts, but they have fire pits all around where they cook food and boil water. Every spring the river floods the dugouts and the soldiers have to sleep in the open on higher ground till the water recedes. They're eaten up with pneumonia, sleepin' sickness, dysentery, diarrhea, and who knows what else. Their bodies are ravaged by chiggers, redbugs, bedbugs, ants, centipedes, spiders, and everything else that creeps and crawls. Soldiers are always scratchin' their heads, necks, and everywhere else they can reach. They got to follow orders all day and have no women to cuddle up to at night. The conditions are so horrible that half of 'em desert their posts each year, and the other half are thinkin' about it.

Accordin' to the corporal who dug the grave, the first shipment of lumber is due to arrive soon, and they plan to use it to build wooden bunks, a supply house, and a horse corral. They've been promised a field oven, and if they don't get it by the end of the year I s'pect there won't be many soldiers left in Dodge come winter.

What I'm sayin', if you're countin' on the soldiers to protect you from Indians and outlaws, they may not be here long, now that the war's over.

CHAPTER 26

AS NIGHT FALLS, I work my wagon into the middle of a large group of travelers—two dozen or more—who've made camp for the evenin'. Few of these families set out together originally, but when families get on the Santa Fe or East-West Trails they tend to form acquaintances and band together in groups. This affords 'em conversation, a helpin' hand, an opportunity to barter supplies, and of course, protection. This bunch is skittish of outsiders, and downright standoffish to find me attemptin' to join their group for the night, especially since I'm haulin' a rottin' corpse, but after I say my name a couple of 'em are impressed, and tell the others how they'd read or heard about the dime novels written about me back East. Of course, that means I have to answer a hundred questions about the West, includin' what to expect from life in Denver, and various other towns in Nevada and California. I make an attempt to talk 'em into settlin' in

Dodge City, but this bunch ain't havin' none of it. They'd made their minds up long ago, so I tell 'em more good than bad, so as not to discourage their dreams. By the time we all turn in I get 'em to promise they'll stop in Dodge for provisions, and some of the men say they'll be willin' to have a drink in our saloon, if Gentry's there.

This is a close-knit group, and although they're all plannin' to settle in different places, I bet they all wind up in the same area, 'cause by the time you've spent two months with a group of people, sharin' meals and conversation, and gettin' to know each other's dreams and kids and livestock, the people you settle down with become more important than the place.

This is a good experience for me, campin' among these tenderfeet, gettin' a chance to witness their future community in the earliest stages of comin' together. I normally camp off to the side of the Trail, away from people, so I can get an early start without disturbin' 'em, but then again I ain't usually drivin' a wagon full of wolf bait. Bein' surrounded by all these people and livestock gives the wolves somethin' else to smell besides Eli's corpse, and the sheer numbers of men and guns offer plenty of protection if they *do* happen to scent him.

Apart from wolves, you know what's really aggressive on the plains?

Insects.

If you think insects are bad wherever you happen to be, you'll want to stay away from the plains when haulin' a leaky corpse. Out of the five types of insects I've already slapped to death on my body tonight the only ones I ever seen before are the mosquitoes, which are as fierce and determined as them you'll find on the White River in August, near Yellville, Arkansas.

And that's sayin' a lot, since them mosquitoes have been known to drive men mad.

I had already moved Louis Hinkle's horse fifty feet from the wagon to give him a break from the stink, but shortly after midnight felt compelled to move him another fifty feet to keep him from goin' blind from the bitin'.

A' course I couldn't even dream of sleepin' amid these conditions, and spent the whole night patrollin' the area and cursin' John Boone and Judge Lobotomy for puttin' me through this unearthly torture in the first place. The smell and bitin' gets so bad I have to pour water from my canteen in the dirt to make mud, which I spread all over my face and hair to give me a layer of protection. Then I force a second pair of gloves on my hands, 'cause the bugs are bitin' right through the first pair. I make a hood outta my wool blanket and wrap it over my muddy head and neck and *still* can't keep the insects from bitin' the shit outta me.

A' course, the group of settlers I'm campin' with are suf-ferin' too, and I feel bad when they abandon their wagons and camps and cluster a couple hundred yards away. I'd love to be with 'em, or at least as far away as they are, but I have to watch for wolves, and can't stray far enough to avoid the smell, which is all-consumin'.

If you puked six gallons of vomit into a shithouse pit and marinated a dead body in it for six weeks it wouldn't smell as bad as whatever's goin' on in the back of Louis's wagon. I've spent time in the most horrific places, among the most primitive people, in the most savage conditions, and never encountered a smell that came close to the one Eli's unleashin' into the world. If you told me Satan was usin' Eli's corpse as a doorway from Hell I wouldn't question it for a second.

I wince as a crawly bug bites me through my blanket, then three mosquitoes bite the wince expression right off my face.

CHAPTER 27

IT'S MORNIN', AND I've stuffed bacon grease in my nose so I can get close enough to Eli's corpse to see what's become of it. When I do, I can tell you it's better and worse than I thought. Worse, because...well, I won't go into it. Let's just say it ain't a pretty sight. And better 'cause the body's surprisin'ly intact, considerin' the hoards of maggots and other bugs crawlin' through his entrails, feastin' on the soppiest parts of his flesh. They're an aggressive bunch, these plains maggots, and I can't help but wonder how much of Eli will be left when I finally get him to Wichita and deliver his remains to the crazy judge who sent me the notice to produce his body.

If I get his body that far.

I'm bringin' that up for a reason. Five reasons, actually, because you know what else is aggressive out here on the plains?

Weather.

Indians.

Outlaws.

Buzzards.

And like I said earlier, wolves.

Right now the weather's clear, though that can change in the space of an hour. While it ain't common to experience wild swings in weather outside tornado season, I ain't the only Kansan who's been sunburned, wind-burned, rained on, hailed on, and frostbit in the same day. As for Indians, outlaws, buzzards, and wolves, I'm apt to run into any, some, or all of 'em today, when I cut from this trail to the East-West Trail. That's a 40-mile stretch where I probably won't encounter a dozen travelers, spaced miles apart. I'll have two rifles and two handguns loaded and near me at all times, and a box of bullets at my feet.

Not to make light of the danger I'm about to face, but the thing that worries me most is Louis Hinkle's horse. He appears to be a sturdy and sensible, but he ain't been battle-tested.

It's nearly five-thirty a.m. and this lazy group ain't even finished breakfast yet, much less cleared a path for me to leave, but I've burdened 'em plenty already, so I hold my tongue as they continue testin' my patience by movin' painfully slow and makin' every attempt to engage me in lengthy conversation. I was ready to leave a half hour ago, havin' done my duties, eaten my breakfast, washed the mud off my face and body, and hitched the horse, but these tenderfeet ain't hardly in motion, so I climb onto the wagon and start maneuverin' it through their campsite. You'd think the stink comin' off Eli would be enough to make 'em scatter their wagons to create an openin', but then again, they might be standin' their ground '*cause* of the smell, hopin' I'll choose a different spot to pass through, while keepin' as far away as possible from their wagons and livestock.

It's like this for several minutes until finally....

Finally....

Someone moves a Conestoga, and I'm on my way.

I trot Louis's horse several hundred yards at different paces to get some air movin' around Eli's corpse. It's a tricky business findin' the perfect speed, 'cause when I go too fast the air blows the stink forward. So I play around with it till I get the stink goin' backwards, which is a welcome enough change to let me realize how bad my neck, back, hips, shoulders, arms, and hands hurt. Most of them pains couldn't be helped, since they're part and parcel of wagon-ridin', but I'm vexed about my arms and hands hurtin' 'cause I know exactly how that happened: I carelessly held the reins the same way all day yesterday, which was stupid on my part. I reckon I was so bored and miserable I didn't think about it till just now.

And while I'm in a complainin' mood I may as well mention my headache, which is the result of not drinkin' enough water last night. At least *that's* easily cured. I take a few swigs of water from one of my canteens and settle in for the long, dangerous ride ahead. Though I find myself yawnin' twice a minute, I'm eager to put eighty miles on the wagon before makin' camp tonight on the East-West Trail. While that's an ambitious goal, it's doable, if I manage to avoid any bad developments.

I've got a plan for Eli's body tonight. I figure to cover him in mud, then put my blanket over him, and cover *that* with mud. Normally I wouldn't give up my blanket, but Eli's stench has already ruined it, so....

Wait.

Off to the right, in the far distance, somethin' catches my eye. I point my buckboard toward it to get a better look, hopin' it ain't a big enough problem to delay my trip, but the closer I get the more I'm convinced it's a woman and young man in need of help. They're far enough from the main trail that no one's noticed 'em yet, or if they have, were too afraid to offer help. I can understand why a family might not want to venture a mile off the Trail to offer help to a stranger, since that's a good way to get ambushed, even at dawn, but anyone with a lick of compassion who sees a woman and boy standin' in the middle of nowhere, wavin' a white shirt, ought to do what they can, even if it's just to make sure the man of the family ain't sick or hurt.

Turns out he's dead.

CHAPTER 28

THE MAN OF the family didn't *just* die, accordin' to Ida Bain, his widow. He was killed two days ago, on the East-West Trail, and she and her son burned his body and kept goin'. Someone told her to cut through to the Santa Fe Trail, and though it weren't the safest place they pointed out to do so, she made a damn good job of it, till she woke up this mornin' to find their horses stolen.

"I'm surprised you weren't killed," I say. *Or raped and kidnapped*, I'm thinkin'.

"We have a shotgun," she says, as if that makes a difference.

"How far away is your wagon?"

"A mile or two."

"I hope you've got the shotgun nearby."

"Why?"

"'Cause if you left it in your wagon, it's probably stolen by now. The wagon *and* the shotgun."

The boy says, "I can get it quick enough."

I s'pect he's tellin' the truth. The grass is high enough that his shotgun could be two feet behind him on the ground and I'd never see it. I say, "You'd be wise to pick it up and head back to your wagon, assumin' it's still there."

"Will you escort us there in your wagon?"

Up to now I've been facin' her and her boy, which means me and the wagon seat have been blockin' their view of Eli's corpse. But now she's pickin' up the scent, and scowlin'. She angles to the side to get a better look at the wagon.

"How'd your husband die?" I ask.

Ida starts to answer, but her friendliness vanishes the moment she spies Eli's body in my wagon. She says, "I'd rather not talk about it."

"I ain't askin' just to make conversation," I say. "I'm the Sheriff of Dodge City, Kansas."

She gives me a doubtful look. Says, "I don't mean to be impertinent, but I strongly doubt you're the sheriff of anything."

"Why's that?"

"You're not wearing a badge."

"We don't actually do that out here."

"Of course sheriffs don't wear badges 'out here'," she says, with great annoyance. "I should have assumed it from the start, since wearing a badge would make a modicum of sense. And if I've learned anything in this God-forsaken country, it's that *nothing* makes sense." She pauses, and eyes me carefully. "Then again, your comment is exactly the type I'd expect to hear from a man who's *impersonating* a sheriff, attempting to gain our trust."

I take a deep breath, let it out slowly. "Well, if that sheriff impersonator's from around here, I'd say he's done his homework, since I ain't never met a lawman west of the Mississippi that wore a badge."

Her son's pointin' a handgun at me.

It didn't come as a surprise.

While she was talkin' a moment ago, walkin' to my right, tryin' to draw my attention, I saw him take two steps back. A second later I saw him kneel into the tall grass, and come up quickly with the handgun. I knew what he was up to from the get-go, and could have easily shot him before he grabbed his gun, but I weren't concerned then, and ain't concerned now. But I *do* say: "Tell your son if he cocks that gun I'll shoot him."

She says, "I sincerely doubt you can secure your gun and fire a shot before he can shoot you."

"You'd best believe I can, and though I'll try my best not to kill him, it'll be a tricky shot, since I'm sittin' on a buckboard, and don't have reason enough to trust this horse. Son, if you'd like a bit of friendly advice on gunfightin', I'll start by sayin' you should stand sideways, to present a narrower target."

He blushes, and turns sideways.

"That's better," I say. "But see how far your arm's extended? It's gonna take you some time to reach up with your thumb to cock your gun. And you can't do that without bendin' your elbow. And when you bend your elbow your gun will be aimin' upward and to the left, which gives me all the time I need to grab my gun and put a bullet in your rib cage. If you've never been shot you can't imagine how bad it'll hurt, or how long it'll take to heal. Not to mention them types of wounds are prone to infection, which causes death more often than not. But like I say, the pain's intolerable, 'cause that bullet's gonna shatter one of your ribs and send dozens of tiny pieces of it through your innards such that every time you shift your weight or cough for the rest of your life you're gonna feel them rib splinters cuttin' into your insides. And the biggest chunk of rib will likely prevent the bullet from passin' out your body, which means my white-hot bullet is gonna sit there, boilin' in your chest, till your blood finally cools it off. And if that's not enough—whoa, son! Don't make that adjustment to your arm just yet, 'cause if you do I'll know you truly intend to shoot me, and I'll have no choice but to react accordin'ly. By the way, I thought you claimed to have a shotgun."

"The handgun was closer."

Ida looks at her son and says, "Keep your gun on him, but don't cock it unless you have to." She takes a step closer to me and says, "I need to tell you something privately."

"Ma'am?"

"I need to whisper something to you. It's important, but I don't want my son to hear."

I frown, knowin' exactly how she expects this to play out, but the whole situation's perplexin'. Ida Bain don't seem like the type a' woman that'd attempt to ambush a complete stranger, but I say nothin', and remain fascinated, wonderin' how far she'll take things before her son tries to cock his gun.

She positions herself behind me and motions me closer.

"Face me, Sheriff. You won't regret it."

I start turnin' to face her, then several things happen at about the same time: I see the shadow of her son's arm bendin' to cock his gun, so I jump from the wagon while grabbin' mine. Her son fires a shot at the exact spot where I'd been sittin' a second ago, but now I'm on the ground, ten feet from him, which allows me to get off a clean shot that hits the side of his handgun and sends it flyin' from his hand. Ida screams and runs toward me, as if she's gonna attack, so I point my gun at her arm. Just as I'm about to squeeze the trigger she changes course and runs toward her son, to make sure he's okay.

I turn my gun toward both of 'em and make 'em lie face down. When they do, I walk closer and tamp down the grass all around 'em, askin', "Where's the shotgun?"

At first Ida says nothin', so I cock my gun and hold it to her son's head.

"Ten feet behind you," she says.

I walk till I find it. Then pick it up and say, "That was uncalled for. I was only tryin' to help you."

"May we stand?" Ida says.

"I reckon."

She gets up, dusts herself off, and says, "I assume you've ruined our handgun?"

"My bullet did."

"Wonderful," she says, sarcastically. "Another nail in our coffin."

"Ma'am?"

"Apart from your inability to adequately identify yourself, you're driving a buckboard with what appears to be a severely decomposed body, which I can only assume belongs to your most recent victim. Is it your intention to ride around with our bodies after killing us?"

"No ma'am."

"Well that's a small comfort, I suppose."

"I ain't plannin' to kill you at *all*."

"I see. So we're simply to be robbed and left to fend for ourselves?" She sets her jaw. "Very well, we're certainly in no position to argue. May I at least ask what you're calling yourself today?"

"Sheriff, same as every day."

She shakes her head. "Of course you are. Why would I even question why a sheriff would want to haul a rotting corpse on a church-style buckboard 50 miles from the nearest settlement? But that's not what I asked. I was referring to your name. Have you chosen one for this particular caper?"

"Emmett Love."

"*Love?*" She gives me a dirty look. "Utterly shameless! Chosen, no doubt, to foster trust from unsuspecting widows. Why not go all out and call yourself Bill *Trust*, or Bob *Hope?*"

"Bob Hope?"

She sighs. "Forget it." She glances at the position of the sun and says, "Look. Apart from losing our horses, this is our first official western robbery, and if you don't mind my saying, I'm finding it ponderous. My son and I have a very difficult day ahead of us."

"Ma'am?"

"I'm saying I wish you'd just get on with it, so we can look forward to the next slice of gristle the Lord intends to serve us as penance for undertaking this absurd journey."

I look at the boy. "Will you tell your ma I'm only tryin' to help you?"

"I think she knows," he says. "She's just upset."

"Where's your wagon?"

He turns and points. "A couple miles."

"Why'd you stop for the night after gettin' this close to the Trail?"

"It was dark. We didn't know how close we were."

"You couldn't spot the fires?"

"No sir."

"Were you among the brush?"

"Pretty much."

"Take me to your wagon."

Ida says, "If you were a gentleman, you'd offer us a ride."

"If I were a gentleman, I wouldn't know better."

"What's *that* supposed to mean?"

"You might be leadin' me into an ambush. If you are, I'd rather have you in front of me, 'stead of in my wagon."

"That's ridiculous."

"Is it? Because I find it awfully hard to believe you'd stop two miles from the Santa Fe Trail, claimin' it's too dark to travel, while claimin' you couldn't see all them fires the Easterners light when they settle in for the night. Once you saw the fires it would've taken you no more than 20 or 30 minutes to go the extra distance, knowin' you'd be campin' in a much safer place."

She huffs and says, "Well pardon us for not knowing the things that are so obvious to those who live here."

She starts walkin', her son at her side. As we move slowly through the high grass he says, "Sheriff Love? Thanks for not shooting me."

"You're welcome, son. I hope you don't make me regret it."

"I won't." He goes quiet a minute, then says, "We're from Charleston. Yankees showed up one morning, burned our house to the ground, destroyed our farm, stole every last cent we had. My father borrowed what money he could, bought a wagon, horses, provisions; planned to move us as far away from civilization as possible. But like she said, he died two days ago. I'm Tom, by the way."

"Thomas," Ida corrects.

"How old are you, son?"

"Fifteen."

"No offense ma'am, but the boy's right. He'll fit in better as a Tom than a Thomas."

Ida says, "I almost wish you *would* rob and kill us."

"Ma'am?"

"I'd prefer it to your tedious conversation and lack of industry. We're wasting time walking when we could be riding."

"You shouldn't have tried to shoot me."

Tom says, "I wasn't going to shoot you. I only wanted to get my gun cocked so you wouldn't be able to shoot *us*. Are you really a sheriff?"

"I am."

"Have you ever killed anyone?"

"I've killed them that deserved it."

Ida says, "That's a convenient way to justify murdering the Lord's children."

We continue in silence for about two miles till we come to their wagon, which has been overturned.

"*Damnit!*" Ida says. "What *next?*"

Tom starts runnin' toward it, till I holler at him to stop. He does, and walks back.

Ida says, "This happened after we left to find help."

I stare at the wagon and frown, thinkin' this whole situation ain't right. I wonder if someone else might be makin' Tom and Ida lure victims from the Trail to this secluded area.

Ida says, "So tell me, Sheriff Love—or whatever your name is—do you intend to sit idly all afternoon, or might you eventually climb off your backside and actually *extend* the help you've promised?"

"Well a' course I aim to help you. I'm just tryin' to decide how serious your troubles are before I start."

She gives me one of the sourest looks I've ever seen on a woman's face that weren't already horrifically deformed. "My husband's dead," she says. "Our horses are stolen. Our wagon's overturned. What little money we had in the wagon has no doubt been confiscated, and our provisions upended, scattered, stolen, or rendered unusable. My son and I are all alone in the world, in the middle of nowhere, with no assets beyond a broken wagon. How serious do things have to be to merit your services?"

I look at the wagon. It's not fancy or big, like a Conestoga. Just an ordinary farm wagon with a canvas cover, lyin' on its side. I ask, "Is someone hidin' in your wagon?"

"Of course not."

"Is that your last word on the matter?"

"It is."

I aim my gun at the canopy, cock the hammer. Then look at Ida and Tom. When they don't move to stop me, I fire two shots.

Ida says, "Thanks for the bullet holes. If it ever decides to rain in this country—which I doubt—I'm sure the leaking canopy will serve to make our trip even less enjoyable. With that behind us, I can't wait to see what other help you intend to give us."

"How'd your husband die?"

"Eagle got him," Tom says.

"Excuse me?"

CHAPTER 29

"MY FATHER WAS bald," Tom says. "He was squatting in the bushes, moving his bowels, when an eagle dropped a large turtle on his head."

"You hear a scream?"

"No sir."

"You saw the eagle?"

"No sir."

"Your ma said you met someone shortly after it happened, and they told you to travel in this direction?"

He nods.

"Is that the same person who told you about the eagle?"

Ida says, "You don't believe it?"

"I've known eagles to drop turtles and armadillos on rocks to break their shells, and heard of bald men bein' killed by turtles dropped on their heads from high in the air.

But it ain't as common as you might think, and in any case that ain't what happened to your husband."

"How can you possibly say that? You weren't there. Not to mention it's the only explanation that makes sense."

"Why's that?"

"My husband's skull was cracked open, there was no one around, and the turtle that struck him was lying beside him, on its back."

"You saw the turtle?"

"I just said that, didn't I?"

"Yes ma'am. But if this happened two days ago you can't have traveled very far. You would've spent time mournin' your husband, and since you burned his body you would've waited till the fire went out before speakin' words over him."

"Is there a point to be made from all this chatter?"

"There is, and I'm gettin' to it. I know this country like the back of my hand. Eagles know it, too, and they ain't likely to mistake a man's bald head for a rock if there ain't no other rocks in the area."

"What are you suggesting?"

"I ain't suggestin' nothin'. I'm sayin' you've been lied to."

She sneers. "All this because Kansas eagles know where rocks reside?"

"That, plus the fact that no Kansas eagle would fly away from its food. It would've come for the turtle."

"You seem so smug, sitting there, making your pronouncements, as if you're the only one who understands nature. But you're not accounting for the most important part of the story."

"What's that?"

"The eye-witness."

"Do tell."

"That shut you up, didn't it?"

"Tell me about him."

"Her."

"A *woman* saw this happen?"

Ida smiles as if she's won some sort of victory. "That's right, Sheriff, a *woman*—a young *lady*—saw the whole thing. *Now* what have you got to say?"

I remove the shells from the shotgun and put 'em in my pocket. Then climb off the wagon and strap on my holster and put one of my guns in it. Then tuck the second gun in my belt, pick up both rifles and carry one in each arm while walkin' a wide circle around Ida's overturned wagon. When I get back to where I started, Ida says, "*Well*, Sheriff?"

"Your problems are worse than you think."

She frowns. "What do you mean?"

"They're plannin' to kill one of you."

CHAPTER 30

IDA ASKS A question, then asks four more before I have time to answer the first one. I believe they were: "Who are you talking about? What evidence do you have for making such a wild accusation? What do you mean they plan to kill one of us? Which one?" and: "Why?"

Instead of answerin', I lead her to the spot where I found the loose dirt.

"What's this?" she says.

"Either your grave or Tom's. She must've dug it when you left to get help."

"She? Who are you *talking* about?"

"The young lady who told you she saw your husband get hit on the head by a turtle and pointed you in this direction—which weren't your safest cut-through, by the way."

"That's preposterous. The 'woman', as you call her, was only fifteen years old."

"Did it strike you as odd a fifteen-year-old girl would be travelin' alone in this type of country?"

"No."

"Why not?"

"I was quite upset at the time, having come upon my husband lying dead with his pants around his knees, and grateful to learn what happened. The girl said her parents were several miles ahead of a group of wagons that were going to cut through to the Santa Fe Trail. They sent her to wait for the other wagons so she could show them where to cut through. Then she pointed the way for us. She was a *child*, Sheriff, younger than her years. I could tell within minutes she was young and innocent."

"I reckon she weren't too young or innocent to kill your husband."

Ida's jaw drops.

"My husband was a large, strong man."

"She had the element of surprise. Snuck up on him and bashed his head while he was takin' a shit."

"She couldn't have been strong enough to kill him with a turtle."

"She hit him with some sort of weapon, then hit him again with the turtle to cover it up."

Ida shakes her head. "If this is how crimes are solved in the West I'm even less keen to continue our journey."

"Ma'am, you'll be lucky to get out of here alive. What you need to do is grab whatever supplies you can salvage from your wagon while I stand guard. As soon as you're ready—and it needs to be *very* soon—you and your boy can climb in the wagon and we'll get the hell out of here."

"Do you seriously believe I'm going to abandon my *wagon?* It's the only asset I have."

"*Fuck* your wagon!" I say.

She stares at me with wide eyes as if shocked beyond belief. But when I say, "*Move your asses!*" they run to the wagon, search frantically, and come back with hardly nothin'.

"We're cleaned out," she says, with tears streamin' from her eyes.

"Well, at least you're both alive. Get in my wagon."

Before they have a chance to, I spot a young woman in the distance, on a roan mare, headin' in our direction, leadin' a horse.

"It's her!" Tom says. "And she's brought one of our horses!"

I normally don't shave when I'm travelin' across the plains, and it's a good thing in this case, 'cause I'm so perplexed my beard stubble gives me somethin' to rub while I'm ponderin' why on earth this young killer girl would take the time to fetch their horse instead of sneakin' up on 'em with a group of bushwhackers.

Then I realize she's probably comin' toward us from that direction while the bushwhackers sneak around and shoot us in the backs. I stand on the wagon seat and scan the area around and behind me even though I'm makin' myself a big target.

But I don't see nothin'. No people, no tall grass movin' or bendin', no nothin'.

Ida says, "I think your theory about the girl is completely wrong. I thought as much even as you were telling it."

"Why's that?"

"You assumed she watched us leave the wagon earlier this morning, and was alone. If she was watching us, all alone, who stole our horses?"

"The gang she's travelin' with."

"Why didn't they just kill us when they had the chance?"

"I ain't sure. Maybe they were concerned about your shotgun. I reckon they made off with the horses and left her here to watch you. They're probably close enough to hear me talkin' right now."

"If that's true, why would she ride into our camp?"

"I ain't sure. To distract us, maybe."

A few minutes later, the girl rides slowly into camp, gives me a close look and a friendly smile and says, "Miss Ida, we're camped a couple miles east. One of your horses found us." She glances at the wagon. "What happened?"

I quick-draw my gun and shoot her through the heart.

Ida and Tom scream as she falls to the ground.

I shout, "Grab the horses and ride out of here the way we came! *Now!*"

They don't move a muscle, just keep screamin'.

I sigh, and wait for 'em to calm down enough so I can explain why I killed her.

CHAPTER 31

"REASON I KILLED her," I say, "She was a Jessie. Now get on the horses. You're lucky to have 'em."

"I'll want my shotgun," Tom says. "And the shells in your pocket."

I give him a look.

He explains, "How else will I be able to protect us?"

"What's a Jessie?" Ida says.

"I'll tell you when we get to the trail." To Tom I say, "I'll hold your shotgun till then, 'cause you'll ride safer holdin' the reins with both hands." To both of 'em I say, "I advise you to ride ahead to the place we met, plus one mile, which will put you in the middle of the Santa Fe Trail. I'll meet you there quick as I can, and give you your shotgun and enough supplies to get to Dodge City, where my wife will take care of you."

"*You* have a *wife?*" Ida says, as if that might be the craziest thing imaginable.

"I do."

"What's her name?"

"Penelope," I say, immediately wonderin' how that name popped out of my mouth. I shake my head. "I meant to say Gentry."

"Is it possible you're married to two women?" she says.

"Well, I married Gentry thinkin' Amy was dead."

"Who's Amy?"

"My first wife."

"Who's Penelope?"

I sigh. "I ain't sure why I said her name."

"So there's no Penelope?"

"She's a real person, just not my wife."

"Whose wife is she?"

"That ain't important. We need to get goin'."

"You know what I think?"

I sigh again. "Nope."

"I think you're planning to steal our wagon."

"You'd be wrong. I'll be right behind you."

She says, "I doubt that." She looks at the dead girl, then back at me. "I think we'll be fine without your help. You should ride to wherever you were heading before we flagged you down."

"What are you plannin' to do?"

"Use the horses to right the wagon. Then hitch them up and head to Colorado...*after* we bury the poor child you murdered in cold blood."

"That's a bad plan, Ida."

"My mind's made up."

"Do you understand your lives are in danger?"

"Our lives were in danger the day we left Charleston. I'm not leaving this wagon behind, Sheriff."

"We don't have time to hitch it."

"You should go, if you're that afraid. But Tom and I are staying." She stiffens up. "We shall *not* be moved."

"You'll be moved all right."

"It's our choice. And it's final."

"Tom?"

Before answering, he looks at the dead girl, then at Ida. "I should stay with my mother."

I look at Ida. "You're killing him."

"I doubt that. Goodbye, Sheriff."

I stare at 'em a long moment, then shrug. "Suit yourself."

I remove the shotgun shells from my pocket and throw 'em toward their wagon. Then say, "To make sure you don't shoot me in the back, I'll ride a half-mile before droppin' your shotgun behind me." I pause. "I'll say one last time I think you're makin' a big mistake."

"It's ours to make," she says.

"Well, I'll wish you all the best."

I start to leave, then stop and say, "I ought to give you an idea what you're in for."

Ida says, "Brace yourself Tom. I feel another speech coming on."

I frown. "The Jessies are a pack of man-hatin' women who live together in a settlement ten or twelve miles west of here, called Mooney Ridge. No one knows how many women live there, 'cause they bury their dead in unmarked graves at night to keep the Indians and outlaws from knowin' their true numbers."

"That's quite a story, Sheriff. And I don't believe a word of it."

"You'd better, 'cause they routinely kidnap young men of your son's age and bring 'em to the settlement for breedin' purposes. That might sound like a good time for you, Tom, but after you've fathered your third or fourth child they'll kill you for three reasons: One, they hate men. Two, food's scarce. And three, they want fresh bloodlines."

"That's preposterous!" Ida says.

I give her a look. "That loose dirt I found near your wagon was meant for you. And frankly, I'm surprised they took the time to dig it, since they usually eat the women they kill. But I'm glad I saw that, 'cause it tells me they've got enough food at Mooney Ridge for the time bein'."

"So we're supposed to believe these Jessie women are modern-day *cannibals*? This is beyond absurd! I've never heard such a ridiculous story in all my life! It's either a legend or a lie, and I doubt you'd know the difference. But here's what I *do* know: this young lady rode into camp with a smile on her face and our horse in tow, and you shot her without so much as asking a question. You had no way of knowing who she was."

"She's a Jessie all right. She's got the brand on her left wrist. Be sure to look at it, 'cause you're gonna see that mark again, and soon. Make no mistake: they're *gonna* kill you, and they're gonna haul Tom off to Mooney Ridge, and that's a fact. Unless someone else comes along and kills you before the Jessies show up."

"If you really believe all this you should return our shotgun now. Otherwise, you're leaving us completely vulnerable."

"You make a good point, but Tom's already pointed a gun at me, and I'd prefer not to give him a second chance, especially when my back's the prime target. I'll ask you one last time to leave the wagon behind and meet me on the Trail."

"By my count that's the second time you've claimed to say something for the last time. I must say I find it amusing you're terror-struck over a group of starving women. But we're not. I bid you good day, Sheriff."

"Well, all right, then."

I point my wagon toward the Santa Fe Trail and hurry my horse along, thinkin', *Damn right I'm afraid of the Jessies! They're a sneaky, bloodthirsty bunch.* As I ride I take a minute to wonder what made me say Penelope was my wife instead of Gentry. That don't make sense for two reasons: first, Penelope *ain't* my wife, and second, I ain't thought about her a single time since I left Dodge!

After I've gone about a hundred yards Ida shouts, "We won't forget you, Emmett Love! We'll tell everyone we meet that you murdered this girl in cold blood!"

I stop the wagon.

Shit.

I hadn't thought about that.

Of *course* she's gonna tell the Jessies I killed that girl! It's the first thing they'll ask her.

I should turn around, go back and kill Ida and Tom so they won't create bad blood between me and the Jessies. I know that sounds extreme, but they're about to die anyway, and the Jessie death will be much worse than the single bullet I'll give 'em.

I sigh. I can think of a dozen reasons why I ought to kill 'em, and only one reason why I shouldn't: it'd be murder.

Yes, I just murdered the young lady. But she was settin' a trap to kill me and Ida, and kidnap Tom. How sure am I?

I'd bet my life on it.

No question.

...But would I bet Ida and Tom's?

I sorta wish I had the fortitude to go back and kill these tenderfeet, 'cause I know damn good and well the Jessies are gonna wind up in Dodge someday, lookin' for revenge, and this right here is the very moment I've put our young men at risk. I spend another minute tryin' to talk myself into killin' Ida and Tom in order to protect Dodge City, but that idea only works in my brain and not my heart, so in the end I smack Louis's horse with the reins and put more distance between us.

I feel bad I weren't able to make Ida and Tom trust me, though I will say Ida ain't the type that's likely to survive more'n a day or two in the West in the first place. I can't hardly count how many times she said she doubted whatever it was I was tryin' to tell her at the time, and in my opinion, a woman who don't know enough to realize she's in critical danger is already dead.

I get to the half-mile mark without incident, then toss the shotgun onto the ground like I said I would, and get about twenty more yards before hearin' one of the scariest sounds I ever heard in all my years of trail ridin'.

CHAPTER 32

LOUIS'S HORSE HEARS the sound too. He rears up and starts runnin' fit to bust.

I turn to look behind me and see a dozen wolves bearin' down on us faster than Louis's horse can possibly pull this wretched wagon. But I whip his rump anyway, and urge him to do all he can.

In the space of thirty seconds they're practically on top of us! The lead wolf is tryin' to jump onto the wagon, and the others are right on his tail. I'm bouncin' around like crazy, to the point I can't even grab my rifles, since they're bouncin' all over the place too.

I still have the guns in my holster and belt and so I grab the one in my belt and fire six shots, four of which completely miss their marks. Even with all this bouncin' I wouldn't expect to miss four shots, but that's exactly what happened, so I drop the empty gun under the bench seat and grab the other one and shoot true enough to watch four more wolves fall and roll. I probably didn't kill any of 'em, but wounded 'em badly enough to make 'em give up the chase.

Suddenly we hit a hole in the ground that jars the wagon so hard I nearly fall off the wagon. It's then I realize I've lost the reins. They've fallen beneath the wagon and are draggin' the ground below it. If they get tangled up in the horse's legs, we're doomed. But before I have time to worry about that, I hear two loud thumps and realize the worst is upon us: two angry wolves are in the buckboard! They're behind me, snarlin' and growlin' and tearin' at Eli's corpse! One of 'em lunges at me so viciously I dive to the floorboard between the seat and the wagon front, and he jumps on top of me, but I'm still holdin' my gun, and lucky enough to bash his snout. Several teeth go flyin' through the air, along with a trail of blood so thick it looks like a rope. He yelps in pain and turns on me with vengeance, and attempts to chomp my wrist with his huge jaws. Knowin' I ain't got bullets or a chance to avoid another thrust, I hold the gun so he can bite the barrel, which he does, and as he pulls it from my grasp I reach under the seat and grab his nuts and rip 'em right off his belly. He don't like that anymore than you'd expect, but between the pain and startlement he falls backward into the bed of the wagon. I feel supremely lucky to be unbit, but now Louis's horse has started slowin' down considerably, and two more wolves jump onto the wagon bed and growl at me while displayin' arched backs and yellow eyes.

The wagon slows almost to a stop, which is good news, since I'm able to grab one of the rifles. I point it and fire four times and hit all four wolves in the wagon, though none are kill shots. Louis's horse stops altogether, but when he hears the remainin' wolves comin' at him from under the wagon he panics and rears up. If I had the reins I might be able to calm him down.

But I don't.

And anyway, I've got other problems: two of the wounded wolves have decided if they don't do somethin' about me now they might not get a better chance later. They come at me together, but I'm ready. After hittin' both of 'em with kill shots, I shoot the other two a second time for good measure. By this time I'm out of bullets, which is doubly bad 'cause the last two wolves turn away from the horse, come around to the back of the wagon, and jump right in, but only long enough to drag Eli's corpse right off the back and onto the ground, where they attack him like he's still alive. I'm sharin' a wagon with four dead wolves, Louis's horse is rearin' up and thrashin' about to the point the wagon could overturn at any minute, and I finally get my last loaded rifle. I climb over the seat, point the gun at the two remaining wolves, and shoot them off Eli's putrid, mutilated body.

I turn my focus back to the horse and try to decide on the best way to calm him. I could climb off the wagon and come around, or crawl onto one of the hitch poles and reach down and grab the reins off the ground. I don't want to climb onto the hitch pole, but if I get out of the wagon, Louis's horse is apt to run off, and I'll be stranded. Also, if I get out of the wagon and try to reach for the reins I could get run over. So I climb back over the seat and lean onto the hitch pole and work my way to where I'm lyin' on it. At that very moment the horse stops rearin' and starts runnin' again. The good news is I didn't get out of the wagon. The bad news is I'm caught in a bad position, lyin' on a narrow length of wood such that I can't go forward or back, and bouncin' around worse than before. Within seconds I lose my balance and fall beneath the wagon and barely miss gettin' hit by the horse's hooves. And yet somehow....

I manage to grab hold of the reins!

I'm bein' dragged under the wagon through the tall grass, while holdin' onto the reins with all my might, hopin' my body weight will tire Louis's horse enough to make him stop.

And it does.

It takes a couple minutes to crawl backwards under the wagon and stand up, at which point I walk over to Louis's horse, pat his neck, and whisper what a good job he done. Then I get the reins situated properly, reload my weapons, turn the wagon around, and head back to fetch whatever's left of Eli's body, which turns out to be an arm, half a rib cage, and a couple of upper leg bones, all of which are covered with jellied patches of grey flesh teemin' with maggots, centipedes, and God knows what else. I gather Eli up, such as he is, and carry him to the wagon, even as a quart of leaky, stinky, puss-filled liquid spills down my shirt at the neck, along with a hundred wrigglin' maggots.

I shudder with disgust.

When I finally get Eli's remains in the wagon, I strip naked, and shake out every stitch of clothin' to make sure the only thing walkin' around in 'em is me.

Yes, they smell like Eli's rotten corpse, and so do I.

No, I no longer give a damn.

Well, yes I do.

I glance at Gentry's small carpetbag and remember how I argued that all I'd need is one change of clothes.

Should have listened to her.

I take out my second blanket, second canteen, and the small wedge of lye soap I thought to bring at the last minute, knowin' I'd be appearin' before the Wichita judge that ordered me to produce the body.

Judge Lobotomy.

I deliver a silent curse skyward on behalf of that judge for all the foolishness he's put me through. Then I scrub every square inch of my hair, face, and body, then my boots. When I'm as clean as I can get myself, I throw my trail-ridin' clothes away, don my church duds, and head to the Santa Fe Trail, to make arrangements for Louis's horse and wagon, and Eli Shed's corpse.

All this because in an hour or two I'm gonna do somethin' *really* stupid:

I'm gonna go back and check on Ida and Tom.

CHAPTER 33

I CAN'T JUST turn the wagon around, 'cause the Jessies'll hear it comin' a mile away.

I'm sure they've struck by now, but in case they haven't—or haven't killed Ida yet, or run off with her wagon and son—I owe 'em my best effort.

You know what I should've done?

Turned my gun on Ida and Tom and forced 'em to ride with me. We could've tied the horses to the back of the wagon and...

No, that wouldn't have worked. The wolves would've killed the horses.

On second thought, I guess I did the best I could. There's no way to force a woman and boy to ride ahead of me, or even *with* me, unless I'm prepared to shoot 'em for ridin' back to their wagon.

And I know they would have.

Over the next half hour I think on all I said and did and come to the conclusion I probably should've stayed with 'em to face the Jessies. I reckon I would've, had it not been for the fact I'm bound by law to get Eli's body to Wichita, and I couldn't have done that if I was dead.

Do I really think the Jessies would've been able to kill me?

I'm certain of it.

You put me, Ida, and Tom in the middle of a field of tall grass, tryin' to defend a wagon, surrounded by twenty or thirty blood-thirsty Jessies who'll come at us day or night, crawlin' through the grass an inch at a time, and strike from all directions with guns, bows and arrows, knives, spears, or worst of all: firepots—and there ain't no hope of survivin'.

So what's my plan?

I'm gonna ride to the Santa Fe Trail, find a group of people I trust, ride a mile or two with 'em, then pay 'em to take my horse and wagon in return for a horse. I'll tell 'em if I don't return their horse before they get to Dodge they can take the horse and wagon to Gentry, and she'll give 'em fifty dollars in gold for their trouble. After gettin' a horse, I'll double back, tie the horse two miles west of Ida's wagon, and creep through the grass till I see what's become of her and Tom. While I doubt she'll be alive, she could be, and if so I might be able to help her...if I can remain unseen before I strike.

CHAPTER 34

IT TAKES LONGER than I thought to talk someone into tradin' me a horse for my rig, even though it's meant to be a temporary situation. In the end I have to give a twenty dollar gold piece to the head of an eight-wagon wagon train in addition to what Gentry'll give him if I get myself killed.

If all goes well, I'll be done with this Ida and Tom business by dusk, and be able to catch up to the wagon train before midnight.

With all that barterin' behind me, I ride Gus, my rental horse, two miles west of the place Ida's wagon was overturned. Then I tie his legs together till he falls down. I don't like doin' this to a horse, and Gus don't like it neither, which is why he's whinnyin' and thrashin' about the way he is. It ain't right forcin' him to stay on the ground like this, but there ain't no way I can't catch a horse that wants to run off, and Gus ain't mine to lose.

I leave him there, but can hear him expressin' his displeasure for the better part of a mile, at which point the Kansas wind does its job and swallows up his sounds.

I'm crawlin' on my belly, workin' my way closer to where the wagon had been a couple hours ago, when I come to a small hill that grades about ten feet. At the top of this hill I raise my head just high enough to get my eyes above the grass...

And duck back down immediately. I didn't look long, but I saw plenty: ten or twelve Jessies spaced apart in the tall grass, 100 yards from the wagon, which is still on its side, just the way I left it. I didn't stare long enough to see how heavily armed the Jessies were, but what I *didn't* see was Tom or Ida.

And that's a puzzlement.

I edge my way back down the hill and change my direction to keep plenty of distance between me and the Jessies, who appear to be dug in, possibly waitin' for a signal before attackin'. I crawl ever-so-slowly toward Ida's wagon until I'm close enough to see they're all gone: Tom and Ida, both horses, and the body of the young girl I shot.

And now I'm truly confused.

If there's no one here, why are the Jessies hangin' around?

...I get my answer within minutes, when I hear the bangin', creakin', squeakin' sounds that can only be made by a buckboard or wagon.

As the sounds get louder, I realize they're headin' directly toward Ida's wagon, and a likely Jessie ambush. This puts me in a quandary. I can't sit idly by while a wagon of travelers gets slaughtered by the Jessies. On the other hand, I can't kill even a dozen Jessies by myself, not to mention the others who are probably hidin' in the tall grass on the far side of the wagon. I try to freeze the moment in time, think about the sun, the wind, the temperature, how old I am, how I feel. Then I think about Scarlett, and hope she grows into the fine young lady she deserves to become, then I think about Gentry: the good times, the hard times, and the recent bad times. I'm doin' all this because I figure these next 20 minutes will be my last on earth.

I try to picture how Gentry will hear the news. Then feel an overwhelmin' sadness, realizin' she'll never hear it. No one knows where I am, or why. I couldn't tell the wagon master what I was plannin', or he never would've lent me his horse. I'll kill some Jessies, and they'll kill me, and them that survive will leave me to the wolves and no one—not even Shrug—will be able to figure out what become of poor Emmett.

Except....

I wonder if Rose or Scarlett might have some way of knowin'.

I cling to that thought for comfort, as it might keep Gentry from spendin' time and money worryin' about me, or tryin' to find me, or my remains.

Of course, Shrug will want to know exactly what happened. He won't know to come to this area, since it's a few miles from the cutoff he'd expect me to take, but he might double back this way, searchin' for a clue. By then the wolf carcasses will be gone, but most of the bones will probably be there. He'll surely sniff out the clothes I abandoned, and he'll know they were mine.

I wonder if he'll laugh a minute, thinkin' about me bein' covered in Eli Shed's liquid stink.

He'll comb the area, searchin' for signs of what might've happened to me, and when he gets to this spot it would be great if I had five stones I could arrange so he'd know it was me, about to die. Under the stones, I'd put my weddin' ring.

But I ain't got stones, so I take a big chance and pull some grass out and twist it into a small rope. Then I put my weddin' ring in the middle of it and tie it together, and place it on the ground and hope between Shrug, Rose, and Scarlett...they'll find the ring and know I've made my last stand, and met my maker.

A minute after gettin' the ring necklace situated in the grass the way I want it, I can tell the wagon is less than 50 yards away.

And I hear voices.

Four people are talkin', and...as I cock my head to concentrate on the voices...the one I'm hearin' at this very moment...is one I've heard before!

I'd love to raise myself high enough to see what's happenin', but I'm lyin' on my belly in a patch where the grass is particularly thick and tall, and no one knows I'm here. While I don't dare rise up to look, I don't dare not to. So I take a deep breath, and slowly lift my head high enough to see four people in the wagon. Two in front, two in back.

I don't know the man and woman in front, but they're Easterners, and almost certainly married. As for the man and woman behind them, well it's Tom and Ida.

I drop back down and try to piece it all together.

As they pass within 20 yards of the spot I'm hidin', I hear Ida tell her tale of woe about how an eagle dropped a turtle on her husband's head two days ago. Seconds later, when they get to the little clearin', Ida hollers her horses are gone and her wagon's been overturned! –As if this is the first time she learned about it!

It's at this very moment I realize the Jessies have been forcin' Tom and Ida to lure people back to the wagon, and sure enough, within seconds, five Jessies jump out of the grass and overpower the man and woman. They wind up stabbin' the man, but just enough to keep him from puttin' up a fight.

Then things get *really* strange! I literally get the surprise of my life when...

Ida starts tellin' the *Jessies* what to do!

Yup. Turns out she's the leader of the Jessies! And Tom ain't her son, he's her prisoner!

I find that out when she slaps his face and tells him about a mistake he made with the husband and wife. He promises to do better next time, and the five Jessies lead the man and woman away, threatenin' to kill the woman if she don't shut up.

She refuses to, so they slash her throat and start cuttin' chunks of flesh from her body before she hits the ground! I s'pect they'll roast and eat these body parts when they get back to Mooney Ridge. The lady's poor husband is sobbin' his heart out over his wife, and I s'pect they'll feed some of her body parts to him tonight, 'cause that's the type of people Jessies are.

You might wonder how I could just lie here and watch all this take place and do nothin' about it. Well, the truth is, while everythin' was unfoldin' I was tryin' to figure out how all the pieces fit together. And when the Jessies struck, I could tell they weren't plannin' to kill the husband and wife. And when they *did* kill her, it happened so quick it was over before I could have got to my feet.

They weren't gonna kill her, but she wouldn't stop hollerin'.

They warned her, plain as day, but she was outraged, and now she's...dinner.

Why not attack 'em now?

Well, consider the situation: Tom and Ida are to my left, holdin' a gun and shotgun, and there are five Jessies with the man, and at least ten more in the grass 100 yards away who didn't even bother to get involved. In addition, as I said earlier, there could be another dozen Jessies on the *far* side of the wagon who ain't showed their faces yet.

It's one thing to put my life on the line if there's the slightest chance of savin' someone. But throwin' my life away when there's no hope of makin' a difference would be a foolish thing indeed, and terribly unfair to my family, and the citizens of Dodge, who depend on me.

As the five Jessies load the wagon with the lady's body parts, Tom and Ida start walkin' back toward the Santa Fe Trail to lure another stranger or two back to their wagon. I wait till the Jessies put the man on the wagon, and watch them ride off in the direction of Mooney Ridge.

Someday, sooner than later, I'm gonna get a group to-gether: me, Shrug, Sadie Nickers and her gang, and whoever else I can get—and we're gonna go to Mooney Hill and clean out that entire nest of vulturous Jessies.

I let Tom and Ida get a mile away before puttin' my weddin' ring back on. Then I crawl back to get Gus, my rental horse. After untyin' him I ride to the area where I first met Tom and Ida, and sure enough, I find 'em doin' what they did this mornin': wavin' white shirts, tryin' to flag down unsuspectin' travelers.

I come up behind 'em at a full gallop, shoot Ida in the back of her head, and pull Tom onto the back of my horse and ride like hell. Now, on the Trail, flanked by dozens of travelers, we slow down to a walk. I figure it'll take us about four hours to catch up to the wagon train, which gives us plenty of time to talk.

"Why didn't the Jessies attack me this mornin'?" I ask.

"Ida wasn't expecting anyone to come help us that fast, but you saw us the minute we started waving the shirts. By the time we got to our wagon only five Jessies were hiding around it, and they signaled us that the others hadn't got there yet."

"I never saw a signal," I say.

"They're crafty," he says.

"Why didn't the five of 'em attack me?"

"They thought about it, but you were already suspicious, heavily armed, and made us walk in front of you, so Ida signaled them to lay low and wait for the others. When the young girl rode in to distract you, the others were a mile away. She was going to put you at ease while the others got into position. Then, on Ida's signal, they were going to kill you. But you shot the girl and rode off before they could get there."

"When I was a hundred yards away Ida yelled at me, threatened to tell people I killed the girl in cold blood. Was that a trap?"

"It was. She was hoping you'd come back to kill us. If you had, we would've run behind the wagon, and the Jessies would have killed you before you got off a clean shot."

Lucky for me I decided not to go back and kill 'em!

Tom says the Jessies attacked him and his parents, but instead of haulin' him to Mooney Ridge, Ida came up with the plan to make him help her lure settlers to the ambush site. Accordin' to Tom they've been doin' it for days, and are so well-stocked with women to eat, they're now takin' live women back to the settlement, where they'll be tied up, forced to do chores till winter, and be eaten as needed. This way the Jessies won't run out of fresh food like they did last year.

He says they're still breedin' and killin' the men.

"If they ain't killin' the women, why'd they dig up the dirt behind the wagon?" I asked.

"That was actually someone's grave."

"Whose?"

He pauses, then says, "My mother's. She died of dysentery while we were crossing that area, and my father and I buried her there. While we were praying, the Jessies attacked us and took my father to their settlement."

"Well, there ain't much hope for *him*, but at least *you're* safe," I say.

When we catch up to the wagon-master I ask if Tom can travel with 'em, and of course they're thrilled to have an extra man and gun among their numbers. I trade Gus back for Louis's horse and wagon, and check to make sure Eli's body parts are still there. They are, so I've still got a mission.

It's dangerous driving a wagon over the Santa Fe Trail at night, since all the campers are on high alert, but I've lost so much time already I decide to just plow forward and take my chances.

Two hours before daybreak I finally reach the cut-through I consider safest. Louis's horse and I both need some rest, so I give us two hours before startin' the dangerous leg of our journey.

When that starts, I'm on edge for eight hours straight, but fortunately, we experience no setbacks, and late afternoon brings us to the East-West Trail, where, within ten minutes, Eli's corpse is attacked by buzzards. But buzzards are easy to shoot if your horse is steady, and Louis's is, so after I hit the first one the rest fly away.

I ride on till my back can't take no more, and then make camp.

Next mornin' we're movin' before dawn, and sometime around three in the afternoon I pass a sign that says *Welcome to Wichita*. I never seen a welcome sign before, and wonder why no one's stolen the wood yet. Twenty minutes later, I find myself a short distance from the county courthouse. I pull the wagon to a stop, tie Louis's horse to a hitchin' post, and encounter two young men, one of which claims to be a judge.

He don't come straight out and tell me he's a judge. That happens after he races over, flailin' his arms in the air like an owl scarin' off a coyote, while hollerin', "What's the *meaning* of this?" which he says three times before I can even say howdy.

When I tell him I received a court order to appear here he gives me an expression so dour you'd swear his young friend was holdin' a turd under his nose. That's when he tells me he's a judge, and takes me to task for haulin' a corpse that's way beyond what he calls "black putrefaction" through the city square in an open wagon.

I allow a healthy portion of his outrage to go unchallenged before tellin' him I'm only followin' Judge Lobotomy's court order to deliver Eli Shed's body to the county courthouse. He handles this piece of news without arguin', which is probably the result of my serious tone and the gun I'm pointin' at his right eye to help him understand I ain't in the mood to be publicly berated for doin' my job. He apologizes for his rudeness, introduces himself and his friend, Jeffrey Somethin'-or-other, who turns out to be his aide. I can't remember Jeffrey's last name, but the man I'm speakin' to is Judge Andrew Williams. I tell 'em I'm Emmett Love, Sheriff of Dodge City, and he takes me at my word and asks politely if I'd be willin' to holster my sidearm and show him the court order.

I do so, and Judge Williams reads it with a look that gets more and more curious the further he reads. Eventually, he turns the page over to see if there's somethin' else written on the back.

There ain't.

He looks at me and says, "This is a Writ of Habeas Corpus."

"So I'm told," I say.

He looks at the sad remains of Eli Shed. "I'm confused. Is this the body of John Boone?"

"Eli Shed."

He sighs. Just as he's about to say somethin', his friend whispers somethin' in his ear. The judge asks me to give them a minute. I do, and they walk a few steps away and whisper back and forth till they're both smilin', which strikes me as odd. But all Judge Williams says is, "Tell me your story."

"Startin' where? The shootin' or when Shrug gave me the Writ?"

"What do you mean by Shrug?"

"Shrug's my best friend. I'm told his name is Wayne Newton. I know he's Wayne, and he's *from* Newton, Kansas, but I ain't sure that's his last name."

"You've never thought to ask?"

"Nope."

"Why not?"

"He don't talk. At least, not to me. Anyhow, Shrug–Wayne–ran here after the shootin'

to find out when the circuit judge might be available to come to Dodge."

"What do you mean he *ran* here?"

"Shrug was injured as a boy such that he can't ride a horse. He runs errands for me."

"*Literally* runs."

I give him a look and feel like sayin', *Ain't that what I just said?* But I hold my tongue, him bein' a judge and all.

He finally says, "Start with the Writ."

I nod, and tell him how Shrug brought me the Writ of Habeas Corpus, and how only two people in town can read Latin, and one was John Boone, and he said I shouldn't take his word for it, so I went to the school marm and asked her to tell me, and she said she had no legal trainin', but said the words mean produce the body. "Well, the only body I had was Eli Shed, but he'd been hauled off to Fort Dodge to be buried, so I borrowed this wagon and drove it to Fort Dodge, where I had a soldier dig up Eli's body."

I tell him the whole story, leavin' nothin' out, includin' the Jessies, the wolves and buzzards. When I'm finally done he said, "Sheriff, that's the most amazing tale I ever heard."

"It ain't a tale," I say. "It's the God's honest truth."

"I wasn't questioning your veracity, sir."

"My what?"

"I'm saying I believe you, Sheriff. I simply meant it's a remarkable story, and one we're certain our colleagues would love to hear."

"What colleagues?"

"We're having a dinner tonight at the Humbolt Hotel to honor Judge Cleveland. Every law officer, judge, professor, and legal student in Wichita will be there. We—Jeffrey and I—think you should attend the dinner and tell your story."

"I only care if Judge Lobotomy will be there."

"I'm afraid Judge Lobotomy's in Red Star, and won't be back for days."

"Can someone else help me?"

"Come to the meeting tonight and tell your story. The judge who's handling Judge Lobotomy's cases will be there, and I'll make sure he gives you a ruling before the evening's finished."

"Why do I have to tell my story?"

"I've been lobbying for years to remove the Latin from the legal system because of the confusion it causes. Your story will help make my point. So much so, that if you agree to tell it at the dinner tonight, I'll personally escort you to the Humbolt Hotel and pay for your room, dinner, and a hot bath."

"When?"

"Right now. However..."

I look at him.

He says, "When you tell your story, I advise you to leave out two details."

"Which ones?"

"I wouldn't tell a roomful of judges that you shot and killed two women without benefit of trial."

"I done what I deemed right."

"I understand. But some of my colleagues might suggest you had the option to arrest these ladies, or at the very *least*, they might feel you could have *questioned* them before administering their death sentences."

I frown. "Anyone who thinks they can live long enough to have a civilized discussion with a Jessie in Jessie country ain't never been exposed to a Jessie."

"All the more reason not to bring it up," he says. "But do tell them you managed to save the boy. Perhaps you can say that the second time you saw Tom and Ida flagging down settlers you raced your horse toward them, startled her, grabbed Tom and hoisted him onto your horse."

"Well, I *startled* her, for sure."

"Excellent."

I shrug, look at the wagon. "What about Eli?"

"Jeffrey?" he says. "Fetch a constable to guard the wagon and Mr. Shed's remains till further notice." When Jeffrey leaves, he says, "So. Are you ready for that bath?"

"My story's that good?"

"And then some."

I grin. "What time's dinner?"

"Eight o'clock. And Sheriff?"

"Yeah?"

"Please don't point your gun at anyone in the hotel tonight."

CHAPTER 35

I HAD NO idea how sore I was till I try to scrunch my body into the small, copper bath can they put in the center of my room. Though my clothes took most of the damage, I burnt a fair amount of skin while bein' dragged behind the wagon, and the pain from them wounds is makin' my bath less pleasant than it originally sounded. But after I settle in, the water boils most of the stiffness and soreness away, and as it gradually changes from scaldin' to warm, I fall asleep right where I'm sittin'.

When I wake up it's dark outside, and the water's almost cool to the touch. I sit a while longer and think about Gentry and Scarlett, and how I can't wait to see 'em, though I probably won't see Scarlett till the end of the week. There's a light knock at the door, like a lady might make, and I say "Come in," and it *is* a lady, by which I mean a female, 'cause a lady wouldn't proposition me the way this one is doin'.

I tell her I ain't in need of companionship other than what my wife provides, and she tells me her name's Alice, in case I change my mind. I tell her I won't, on account of how I'm married and all, and she asks me what that's like.

"You mean marriage?" I say.

She nods.

"Marriage is sorta like farmin': every day you work like hell, and every night you pray for what you *don't* want."

She cocks her head. "Like what?"

"Well, you'll pray it won't frost tonight, or snow tomorrow. You'll pray the bugs don't come, or the chickens don't die, or the horse don't colic, or the plow don't break, or the rats don't—"

—"*Stop!*" she says, coverin' her ears with her hands. "I *get* it! But how's that like being married?"

"Well, even if you do everything right, you still have to pray she don't run off with someone else, or stop findin' you attractive, or fall out of love with you for somethin' you can't fix."

I let her think on that a minute before askin' what time it is. When she tells me, I realize I've only got twenty minutes to get dressed before the dinner starts!

I throw my clothes on and race downstairs and wind up havin' a helluva dinner. Best I ever had, outside of what Rose used to put together on her massive kitchen table back in Springfield before the war. I don't say much to the men I'm sittin' with, and they don't ask much, since they can tell I'm an ignorant frontiersman instead of a legal expert.

When Judge Andy Williams introduces me I walk to the front of the room and tell the story of how John Boone shot

Eli Shed, and what we learned about Eli, and how he died, and how Shrug ran all the way to Wichita with my report of the circumstances surroundin' the shootin', and how he brought me back a Writ of Habeas Corpus, and how I came to understand what that meant, and how I dug up Eli's body and brought it here.

The more I talked the more they laughed, and I don't know what they thought was so funny, but by the time I finished they were on their feet, laughin' and clappin', and askin' for more stories about Dodge City. I tell 'em a few stories about how we used to put lawbreakers in deep pits in the ground, since we didn't have jail cells, and of course, they all wanted to hear about the time I was ambushed at the *Spur* by the famous outlaws Sam Hartmann and Bose Rennick, and laughed their asses off when I told 'em how Rudy the Bear saved my life that day. I figured out early on they were laughin' *at* me, 'stead of *with* me, but I kept remindin' myself how nice my room is, and how wonderful the bath and dinner were, and how I'd be seein' Gentry in two or three days and how none of this would matter...and by the time I finished, they seemed quite genuine in their praise, and I was treated to several enthusiastic rounds of drinks.

It weren't till after my talk I found out they were laughin' 'cause the Writ of Habeas Corpus meant I was supposed to bring John Boone to Wichita, not Eli Shed.

"Well, does Habeas Corpus mean deliver the body, or not?" I asked.

Judge Williams said it's sort of like a Latin figure of speech.

"Why didn't they just write a normal letter tellin' me to bring John Boone?"

He said attorneys and judges use big words and secret codes like Latin to make 'em seen smarter than they are, and to make regular folk afraid to represent themselves, so they'll have to hire lawyers and such. He said judges also make the attorneys call 'em certain titles like "Your Honor," and even the lawyers call themselves "The Honorable So-And-So" so regular folk will believe they're honest and trustworthy, even when they ain't. He wants to change all that, but says his views are in the minority.

I tell him lawyers and judges have a lot in common with wolves and badgers.

"How so?" he asks.

"When they feel inferior to their prey, they puff themselves up and try to appear more powerful than they really are."

"That's an excellent observation," he says, and adds, "If things continue in this manner, only lawyers will be able to interpret the law. Then, before you know it, lawyers will be running the country. We can't let that happen, or how big a mess will the country be 150 years from now?"

"What year would that be?" I asked.

"2016."

"Well, I reckon neither of us'll be around to worry about it by then."

Before headin' to bed Judge Williams makes Judge Lobotomy's replacement give me the bad news: I have to take Eli's body back to Fort Dodge to be buried, and have to keep John Boone jailed till the circuit court judge comes to Dodge to give him a fair trial.

"When might that be?" I ask.

"Days, months, years...there's no formal schedule."

"*Years?*"

"It's possible. What's happened, the war screwed everything up. We simply don't have enough judges to service the outlying towns. Not to mention when they hear stories like the one you told tonight about how dangerous it is to travel, well...." He waves his hand in the air.

"You mean my story might've made things worse?"

"Probably. Sorry."

I sigh. "Well, it won't be fun takin' Eli back, and I certainly don't look forward to guardin' and feedin' John Boone in my jail cell for months or years. On the other hand, it was a fine bath."

"Well, that's something," he says.

Two days later, 60 miles from Dodge, I come upon a group of settlers standin' in a circle by the far edge of the Santa Fe Trail. I come closer and I see 'em prayin' over four graves. To the right of the graves, a young man has been hanged by his neck from a tree limb. He's dead, and I can tell he shit his pants, the way most hangin' victims do, but what makes this one unique for me is it turns out to be Tom, the boy I saved from the Jessies.

At first I figure the Jessies caught him and strung him up, 'cause when I put Tom with the wagon-master they were headin' west. And now he's 20 miles *east* of where I dropped him off.

But it weren't the Jessies that got him.

Turns out the night they camped, Tom met a young widow who owned a huge Conestoga and a team of six horses. When he learned she was headin' back East after losin' her husband, he sweet-talked her into takin' him with her, and after a day of travel, Tom killed her and her two kids and stole their rig. He might've got away with it, except when he stopped to water the horses, a man and woman pulled over to admire the Connestoga. As the man talked, his nosy wife poked her head into the back of the wagon and saw the dead bodies. She screamed, and Tom stabbed her, but the husband managed to hit him over the head and knock him out. Now he's hanged, and I feel responsible for the people he killed.

I look at his body, swayin' gently in the breeze. It's a pretty day, and this is a peaceful place for the dead to meet their maker, if you can ignore the buzzards circlin' overhead, waitin' for their first chance to pick Tom's sorry bones clean.

I thank the mourners for tellin' me what happened, then remove my gun from its holster and fire two bullets into Tom's dead body, to let him know what I think about what he done to that poor widow and her kids and the nosy lady who stopped to offer help. For the next twenty miles till the time I camp for the night I ask myself: *Why did I save Tom and put him in a position to hurt these poor people? Why couldn't I figure out he was damaged on the inside? What should I have done? And...What's the world comin' to, when a seemin'ly normal young man can turn into this type of monster?*

The next evenin', after deliverin' Eli's remains to Fort Dodge, I finally steer Louis's horse and wagon into the outskirts of Dodge, to find myself besieged by a dozen citizens hoppin' up and down, yellin' and screamin' and racin' ahead of me; hollerin' at the top of their lungs, "Emmett's back!"

I ain't never had this type a' reception and can't help but wonder what the hell's goin' on. My original plan was to go straight to the *Spur* to give Gentry the biggest hug in all the world, but I never get past my office, due to the huge number of people blockin' my way. I reckon ninety percent of the county is clustered in front of my sheriff's office, which makes this the biggest crowd of people that ever assembled in Dodge.

But when I find out what they're *doin'* here, and why they're so happy to see *me*...I wish I'd waited another day before leavin' Wichita.

CHAPTER 36

AS IT TURNS out, the City of Dodge had been holdin' the damn beauty contest all day today, and about an hour ago it came down to two contestants. But who they are, and how it happened, and how I suddenly got involved—requires some explainin'.

The contest started this mornin' at the *Spur*, and our mayor, Margaret Stallings, was the judge. But after a few minutes the women came to the decision they didn't think the judge should be a woman.

Everyone wanted me.

Margaret explained I might not be back for days, and said the contest needed to go on as scheduled.

Then someone said, "How about John Boone? He doesn't know many women in town, so he won't be biased. Not only that, but the contest was his idea in the first place."

Everyone jumped on the bandwagon, but some of the men thought Boone shouldn't be the *only* judge, since he might be overly particular about the women's teeth and smiles, him bein' a dentist and all. So they decided to have two judges, Margaret and John, and since Shrug wouldn't allow John to be removed from his cell as per my orders, the contest was moved to my office, and the contestants had to parade one-at-a-time, through the jail.

That's how it went all through the day, as Margaret and John worked the field of more than 200 ladies down to the final 10.

But then somethin' happened.

Gentry showed up with a plate of biscuits and bacon for John Boone's dinner, and he did a double-take and immediately insisted she enter the contest. He went so far as to threaten to withdraw as a judge if she said no. Someone explained that as Emmett's wife it wouldn't be fair for her to compete, but Boone reminded them I wasn't judging, so there was no reason Gentry couldn't enter.

The people agreed, and talked Gentry into participatin'.

Over the next hour the field of women was narrowed to two: Gentry Love, and Penelope Way.

And of course, Margaret voted for Penelope and John Boone voted for Gentry.

It was a tie.

But the crowd refused to allow a tie, and fistfights began breakin' out among the gamblers who'd voted on havin' a clear result. People were yellin' and carryin' on, and lives were bein' threatened, when into town I rode, and the call went up for me to give the tie-breakin' vote.

Them who sided with Penelope were furious, 'cause how could I not vote for my wife? But them who sided with Gentry were greater in number and when the vote was made, I was elected to break the tie.

Gentry, bein' Gentry, tried to resign from the contest and give the victory to Penelope, but the crowd was havin' none of it.

So here I am, lookin' at Gentry and Penelope, dressed in their finest, and both makin' eyes at me, and I can tell you with total honesty I'd rather judge a beauty contest among the vilest Jessies while eatin' a bowl of Rag Soup— than to be in this position.

I can't imagine Penelope thinkin' the first thought that I'd pick her over Gentry. First of all, Gentry's prettier. So much prettier I can't believe *any* of the gamblers would have bet on Penelope. Then again, if Margaret thought Gentry was prettier, she'd have said so, and I wouldn't be in this position. Second of all, beauty is more than just a pretty face, and in addition to havin' a prettier face—in my opinion, at least—Gentry's got the firmest, finest, womanly figure I ever saw. Thirdly, she's my wife, and I can't imagine the coldness she'd show if I *didn't* pick her. And fourth, the sting of hurtin' Penelope's feelin's would be far outweighed by the warmth Gentry'll shower on me for choosin' her.

The two lovely ladies stand in front of me and give me their best smiles while the crowd cheers encouragement. Finally, Margaret holds up her hand and says, "Emmett, it's time to make your choice."

"They're both as beautiful as can be," I say, "but if I have to choose one over the other, I reckon I'm gonna have to pick...Penelope."

CHAPTER 37

THE CROWD GOES crazy with shock and awe, but all I'm lookin' at is the expression on Gentry's face. I expect her to be angry, hurt, confused, or jealous, but she don't appear to be any of those things. In fact, she's—not exactly, but sort of—smilin'.

I see her tryin' to make her way toward me, 'cause we ain't even had time to hug yet, and I'm tryin' to get to her too, but both of us are swallowed up by the crowd before we have a chance to close the distance between us.

I know why I chose Penelope, but I ain't quite sure how to phrase it to Gentry.

But later on, when we finally *do* get to be together at the Spur, in between takin' drink orders and entertainin' the masses, she gives me the warmest, most wonderful hug and kiss and tells me she understands why I done what I did.

"You had no choice," she says. "You had to take the position you took from the very start: if you're judging the contest, it wasn't fair for me to be in it. Being honest, you had no choice but to vote for Penelope."

"Exactly right," I say.

Gentry adds, "But being a good person, you didn't explain that, because it would diminish Penelope's victory."

"Wow."

An hour passes, and I realize I need to tell John Boone what I learned in Wichita, and why he might have to stay in jail for months or years.

I sneak out the bar, make my way to the deserted sheriff's office, open the door...and find Penelope standin' alone, waitin' for me.

"I love you," she says. She said it simply, without any particular passion in her voice, like it's such an obvious matter of fact it barely needed sayin'.

"I'm honored," I say. "Truly honored. But my heart belongs to...ah..."

"Gentry?"

"Uh huh."

It weren't that I forgot Gentry's name just now, or had trouble sayin' it out loud, it's just that I got sidetracked when Penelope opened her shawl and had not a stitch of clothin' buttoned beneath it.

"I knew you'd pick me," she says.

"You did?"

"There was never a doubt in my mind." She moves toward me and says, "I don't have Gentry's experience, or any real experience at all. But all this is yours, however you want it; whenever it suits you. And Gentry will never have to know. What are you doing?"

"Lighting a lamp."

"There's light enough coming through the windows."

"I want to see."

"You must know I'm shy."

"I need to see."

"Emmett, wait. I've never show my body to a man before."

"What about Oliver?"

"I always undressed under the covers. And got dressed after our...sessions."

I light the lamp.

"I won't stare long," I say. "I just need to...*What the*—?"

I stand there with my mouth hanging open.

She covers her breasts with her arms. "What's wrong?" She starts to panic. "*Emmett?*"

"Please," I say.

"What?"

"Turn around."

"I *beg* your pardon?"

"Please."

She reluctantly turns around. Then says, "What do you intend to *do?*"

"Look at your lower back."

"Why?"

"Just...let me see it."

She pauses. "I've already offered myself to you, so I suppose you might as well pull down my skirt and lift the back of my blouse to your satisfaction. But I'd be remiss if I didn't say this experience is proving less romantic than I anticipated."

"I'm sorry about that."

"It's all right, I'm sure. It just puts me in mind of the time we inspected our mare's fanny and feminine parts prior to having her bred. Except this time, I'm the horse."

I slide her blouse up till I see what I'm lookin' for: three tiny moles a quarter-inch apart, in the shape of a triangle. I must have murmured out loud, 'cause she says, "Is this what churns your butter?"

"No."

"Good," she says. "May I turn around now?"

"You may."

She does, and sees my face. "What's wrong?"

"I've seen this before. And everything else."

"What are you *talking* about?"

"Your body. Your...uh...private parts."

"That's impossible!"

"In my dream."

She sighs. "Emmett?"

"Huh?"

"I don't mean to be forward, but...what about my bosoms?"

"What about 'em?"

"Well...don't you want to...I don't know, *caress* them or something?"

She grabs the front of my pants with her hand—I don't know which one she grabbed me with, nor does it matter, as either would feel as good when rubbin' my pecker—which one of 'em *is*. But unlike what happened years ago with May Gray, I don't let things get outta hand.

In hand, I mean.

What I'm sayin', I back up and tell her to cover herself.

"No, Emmett. We've put this off long enough. If we don't do it right here and now, it's apt to never happen."

"It ain't gonna happen, Penelope. This ain't right. There's somethin' else at work here, and I suspect it's witchery."

"Don't be silly. It's only natural we feel so much heat for each other. Now kiss me. You know you want to."

"I do—which is how I know these ain't my true feelin's. I only want Gentry. But these last few days, every time I see you, somethin' happens."

"I feel the same way."

"I *know* you do."

"This is beyond our control, Emmett."

"I *know* it is. And that's how I know it ain't natural."

"What are you trying to say?"

"I'm tryin' to say I love Gentry."

"I understand that, Emmett. I'm not asking you to *leave* her."

"You deserve better than me."

"I expect you're right. But you're the one I want."

"Button your blouse, Penelope. This can't happen."

"Is there something wrong with my body?"

"No. It's perfect."

"You kissed me last week. You *wanted* me, Emmett. And you chose me over Gentry today."

"I did all them things. But it has to end. Now you get dressed and outta here while I talk to Mr. Boone."

She starts cryin'.

"Aw shit, Penelope."

She's gaspin', tryin' to talk between sobs: "I'm sorry, Emmett...but...you've really...hurt my feelings....Do...you have...*any* idea what it's like to...throw yourself at someone you love...only to...be *inspected*...and found...*lacking?*"

"That ain't what happened. You're beautiful, and you know it."

She sniffs. "Tell me again."

"I won't. Now go home."

She don't move, so I say, "I *mean* it, Penelope!"

She pauses another moment, then gets herself back into her blouse and buttons it up, sniffin' the whole time, then puts the shawl around her neck. As she walks to the door she says, "You'll change your mind, you know."

"I don't think so."

"You will, though. And when you do, I just might have moved on. Think about that."

"I'm sorry, Penelope."

"Me too, Emmett."

I open the door for her and wait till she leaves. Then I pick up the lamp and enter the jail door to talk to Boone. I get as far as sayin' "Howdy," and hear a loud gunshot just beyond the walls. I rush outside and see Penelope Way lyin' in the street, clutchin' her chest. Her body jerks once...twice...then goes limp.

I check her pulse.

She's dead.

CHAPTER 38

I HEAR A sound in the alley. Footsteps, coming my way, and fast. I draw my gun, but before I see anyone I hear a woman's voice: "Emmett? Are you *okay?*"

It's Gentry.

Within seconds she's by my side, starin' at Penelope. "What on *Earth?* Oh my *God!*"

She leans over Penelope's body, puts her head to her chest. "Is she...Oh God, Emmett! I think...Oh *God!* Penelope's *dead!*"

"She just left my office," I say.

We look into each other's eyes and ask the same question at the same time: "Did you do it?"

And we both say no.

By then, five or six others have joined us. I ask if anyone saw the shootin'.

No one did.

But Daisy Leek says she and her husband walked past the sheriff's office minutes ago and saw Gentry lookin' in the window.

"You're mistaken," Gentry says. "I just got here. I was on my way to the sheriff's office to fetch Emmett when I heard the shot."

"You came by way of the *alley?*" I say.

"Yes, of course. That's the way you usually walk home after work, isn't it? Well, I didn't want to miss you. Has anyone seen Oliver?"

Everyone looks around.

No one has seen him.

I say, "Someone go to Miss Gilmore's house. See if he's there."

"Why would he be at Miss Gilmore's?" Daisy asks.

I don't answer.

I look at Penelope's face. Then Gentry's.

Minutes ago this beautiful young woman said she loved me, and now she's gone forever. I don't see anythin' in Gentry's eyes other than concern, but if she really was peekin' through the window, though the curtains were shut, I wonder how much she might've seen?

I get my answer seconds later when Shrug enters the office to fetch the lamp, and I see him clearly, all the way from here. When he comes out I ask if he saw what happened. He signs he heard someone runnin' away, right after the shot.

"Man or woman?" I ask.

He signs he ain't sure.

"Which way did they run?"

He points to the alley on the far side of the street. If he's right, it couldn't have been Gentry.

"Only one thing wrong with that," I say.

"What?" Gentry asks.

"When Penelope left my office she was walkin' toward Second Street."

"So?"

"She was shot in the chest, not the back."

"So?"

"If someone shot her and ran to the far alley, they would've had to *shoot* her, run *past* her, and cross the lit street to get out of sight. The smart thing would be to hide in the alley by my office, shoot her, then turn around and run down the alley."

"But that's not what happened," Gentry says, "Or I'd have seen her."

"Her?"

"Or him. I'd have seen whoever shot Penelope."

I give her a look.

She says, "What was Penelope doing in your office without her husband?"

Everyone looks at me, and though the streets are lit in general, I'm glad it's dark enough that they won't see my face turnin' red, in case it does. I say, "Penelope wanted to thank me for castin' the winnin' vote."

"That's all?" Gentry says.

"Pretty much. She weren't there but a couple of minutes."

She stares straight into my eyes and says, "Maybe we should ask John Boone what he heard."

"I'll do that. Why don't you and Daisy arrange to have Penelope cared for?"

"What do you suggest we do with her?" Gentry says.

"What do you mean?"

"We usually toss our dead in the back of a wagon and haul them off to Fort Dodge. Would you like us to fetch a wagon?"

I give her a stern look. "I don't know, Gentry. It's your call. Treat her however you'd normally treat a proper woman who was gunned down in the street."

"*Proper* woman?" Gentry says.

"Are you two okay?" Daisy asks.

"We're just upset. Gentry and I will go talk to Mr. Boone. Can you make whatever arrangements you feel are appropriate?"

She nods.

As Gentry and I head to my office, Shrug hands me the lamp and waits for us to enter. Then he stands guard so she and I can talk.

When we're alone Gentry says, "You've been hot for her since the day she came to town."

"That ain't true."

"What happened in here tonight, Emmett? And don't lie."

"I won't lie. But I need to ask you somethin' before anyone else does."

"Fine. Ask it."

"Are you carryin' your derringer?"

"I always carry it."

"Let me see it."

"That's not a good idea."

"Why?"

"If you find I'm missing a bullet you might jump to the wrong conclusion."

"*Are* you missing a bullet?"

She sighs, hands me her gun.

She *is* missin' a bullet.

"I didn't shoot her, Emmett," she says. "Do you believe me?"

"I *want* to. Did you look through the window?"

"If I *had*, what would I have seen?"

My turn to sigh. "She opened her blouse to me."

"And?"

"Offered herself. Said she didn't expect me to leave you, but she'd be mine, whenever I wanted. You don't seem surprised."

"When it comes to Penelope, nothing surprises me. Did you accommodate her?"

"What do you mean?"

"Did you *poke* her, Emmett?"

"Of *course* not!"

"Are you sure? Because it would make sense if you fornicated with her, then felt badly about it, and shot her to keep her from telling her friends."

"That's crazy!"

"Is it?"

I hand her my gun. "You see any bullets missin'?"

"You had time to reload."

"No I didn't! And anyway, John Boone and I were in the same room when she got shot. You can ask him, if you want."

"What good would *that* do? He's your *attorney*. Of *course* he'll be your witness."

I frown. "Daisy and Ezra saw you lookin' in the window. If you *didn't* shoot Penelope, you'll need to explain why you looked in the window, and left, then came back."

"It was dark. They can't prove it was me."

"Talk to me, Gentry."

"*Why?* So you can put me in *jail?* So you can watch them *hang* me?"

I'm suddenly worried about how much of our conversation John Boone can hear. So I whisper, "Whether you shot her or not, I won't let anyone harm a hair on your head."

"You swear?" she whispers.

"I swear. Did you do it?"

"No."

We continue talkin' in whispers, startin' with me sayin', "Did you look through the window?"

She nods. "I saw you lift her blouse. Why were you staring at her back?"

"I'll tell you later. What else did you see?"

"When she turned to face you, I saw her tits."

"Did you watch long enough to see me turn her down?"

"No. But if you tell me you did, I'll believe you."

"I did."

"I believe you."

"I believe you too."

"Thank you, Emmett."

"What happened to your bullet? Your derringer holds two. You're *always* fully loaded."

"I honestly don't know what happened to it. I noticed it missing a little while ago."

"When?"

She takes a deep breath. "When I saw you and Penelope carrying on, I was so angry I grabbed my gun and cocked it. But it didn't sound right, so I walked till I found enough light to check it closely."

"You were plannin' to shoot her?"

"I don't know. Her...you...both of you....It crossed my mind. But my gun didn't *feel* right. I didn't want to pull the trigger and have it blow up in my hand."

"Is that the *only* reason you didn't shoot us?"

"I don't know. Maybe."

I think about what Judge Williams told me about the Jessies I shot. Then whisper, "I'd advise you not to tell that part of the story to anyone else. When's the last time you had two bullets?"

"This morning."

"You checked?"

She nods.

"You keep it on you at all times. You've sewn a pocket for it on the inside of all your dresses."

"All but one," she says. "The beauty contest dress doesn't have a pocket! I didn't have my gun during the time I was in the contest. Someone must have gone through my dress and stolen one of my bullets."

"Why would anyone do *that?*"

"I don't know, Emmett, but the bullet's gone, isn't it?"

244

I hand her gun back to her. "You'd better replace it, quick as you can."

She nods.

CHAPTER 39

THIS MORNIN', JUST after dawn, Margaret Stallings orders me to arrest Gentry for Penelope's murder, based on the eye-witness testimony of Daisy and Ezra Leek, who said they saw her lookin' through my window minutes before Penelope got shot. They also told Margaret they heard me admit that Penelope had been in my office and left just before gettin' shot, and said they heard Gentry confrontin' me about it in a harsh tone while she was kneelin' over Penelope's body. Margaret personally dug the bullet out of Penelope's chest and declared it to be the same type of bullet that's most common to derringers, of the sort Gentry owns.

Now, in the jail, I ask John Boone if he'll represent Gentry. He says he can't, since he's a witness for the prosecution.

"How can I get Gentry out of here?"

"By winning her trial."

"It could be months or years before a judge shows up to give her a trial. It wouldn't be right to keep Gentry locked up that long."

Boone gives me a surly look. "It would be easier not to take that remark personally if you'd shown a similar compassion for *my* situation."

"I feel bad for you, too. But I saw you shoot a man in an unprovoked situation."

"There's a story floating around town that you shot a young woman who did nothing worse than ride into your camp with a horse she found."

"That ain't even close to bein' true."

From the cell next to Boone's, Gentry says, "I didn't shoot Penelope."

"I believe you on your looks alone," Boone says. "And if it makes you feel better, you won't have to be here more than a day or two."

"What do you mean?" I ask.

"I've talked Mayor Stallings into holding an inquest."

"What's that?"

"Something you could have done for me, had you not sent your friend to Wichita with the details of my case."

"I don't understand."

"Of course you don't." He puffs up like a politician, about to make a speech. Then says, "The Constitution grants all citizens the right to a speedy trial. However, we're living in post-war Dodge, which is little more than a frontier outpost, and, as you learned in Wichita recently, the state is currently experiencing a serious shortage of judges.

Therefore, it behooves us as a community to adjudicate such matters as we can, based on precedent, whenever possible."

I give him a look. He explains, "In a case such as this, instead of waiting for a certified judge to make a formal ruling based on a strict legal interpretation of—"

"I have no idea what you're talkin' about. All I asked is what's an inquest?"

"An inquest is a judicial inquiry. I talked Margaret into holding one in order to determine Penelope's cause of death."

"Well, that's a waste of time. Everyone knows she was shot in the chest."

"Yes, but by *whom*? Since there's no eye witness to the shooting, the purpose of Margaret's inquest is to determine if there's sufficient cause to arrest *Gentry* for Penelope's murder."

"Margaret ain't a judge."

"True. But as mayor, she's the highest-ranking county official, and the *only* official we're likely to have available in the months to come. It's my opinion—and now Margaret's—that in the absence of any higher authority, she has the right to declare herself a *de facto* judge with regard to most civil and certain criminal matters."

"What's that mean?"

"It means we believe she has the right to decide if Gentry—or someone else—or no one—will have to be incarcerated until a judge shows up to hold a trial on this matter."

"Can she declare a person innocent or guilty?"

"In my opinion, no. But if she rules there's insufficient evidence to hold someone in custody there probably won't be a trial."

"Why not?"

"Unless new evidence comes to light, I doubt the circuit judge will want to devote much time to an old case the community deemed unsolvable."

"So all we have to do is convince Margaret that Gentry didn't do it?"

"That's all you'd have to do. However, you should be forewarned that I'm planning to testify on behalf of the victim."

"How can you testify about anything that happened? You were locked up when she was shot."

"Quite true, but I heard plenty."

"Like what?"

"Like everything you and Penelope said to each other before she departed the premises."

"You're plannin' to *tell* all that?"

"I am."

"In *public?*"

"If asked, I'm *required* to, by law."

"You'd destroy her reputation."

"Nevertheless, it's my duty to tell what I heard. Especially when it speaks to motive."

"*What* motive?"

"Gentry's been placed at the scene of the murder, prior to the shot. She was seen looking in the window. My testimony will explain what she would have seen. And based on what I heard, Gentry had plenty of motive to shoot Penelope."

"What *else* did you hear last night?"

"If you're referring to your conversation with Gentry, you'll have to wait till I'm called to testify at the inquest."

Gentry says, "Emmett?"

I look at her.

"You can't possibly expect me to squat over this chamber pot to do my business in the presence of Mr. Boone."

"You need to squat now?"

"Not yet, but soon."

"I'll avert my eyes," Boone says.

"That ain't good enough," I say. "I'll escort you to the outhouse."

Boone says, "I hope you don't expect me to hold my water all day and night until you happen to be available to escort *me* to the outhouse!"

I frown. "That's exactly what I expect."

"Well, that's unreasonable. You really should let me go, Sheriff. It's ridiculous to keep me locked up for months or years waiting on a trial that's going to result in my innocence anyway. With Gentry locked up the next day or two, you'll have to find someone to feed us. And what about my clients? I can't discuss legal strategies in front of your wife. You'll have to put her someplace else while I'm conferring with clients. And what if you have to arrest a third person? Is it fair to put them in the same cell as me or Gentry?"

"They'll be in *your* cell, fair or not."

"I hope for your wife's sake they turn out to be gentlemen. But in my experience, jailed men aren't predisposed to chivalry."

I scowl just thinkin' about what Gentry might be exposed to. I ain't so worried about the next day or two leadin' up to the inquest, but I dread all them months or years from now, if Margaret finds her guilty enough to stand trial. Durin' that time I'll likely arrest dozens of the hardest men who ever roamed the plains. How can I possibly house them in the cell next to Gentry? How am I goin' to arrange all the pissin'—and shittin'—the prisoners will need to do every night and day? Who's gonna *feed* all these people day after day if Gentry's locked up?

Gentry knows me well enough to know what I'm thinkin' most of the time, and this ain't no exception. She says, "Well, you always wanted this jail."

"Yeah, I did. But it's turnin' out to be nothin' like I expected. Let's go visit the outhouse."

CHAPTER 40

THERE AIN'T BUT a fraction as many people at the inquest today as there were at the beauty contest two days ago, which says a lot about what most folks consider important. Up to now I always considered Margaret to be a close friend, but she came down on me pretty hard, makin' me testify about all the things John Boone heard me and Penelope say to each other.

That was really embarrassin', and there were lots of shocked faces.

There was also a good amount of snickerin' at the mention of Penelope's bosoms and her inexperience, and how I made her turn around, and what she said about it, and so forth, and I found myself wishin' more than once that John Boone had a shorter memory for detail.

I come off lookin' like a decent man and faithful husband till Boone testified hearin' me admit I kissed

Penelope last week, and heard me say I'd wanted her in a physical way, and dreamed about her, and told her she was beautiful, and her breasts were perfect, and her body was exactly the way I dreamt it, includin' her lower back.

To my dyin' day I'll never forget the hurt in Gentry's face when I publicly owned up to sayin' all them words to Penelope.

But Boone also told the good things I said about Gentry, includin' how I loved her, and how she was the only one for me, and how I weren't gonna let Penelope give herself to me. All in all, I probably came across better than most men would have done, had a woman like Penelope thrown herself at them, and the proof is in the eyes of nearly every woman in the room. They seemed transfixed by every confession I made, and looked at me the same way Penelope did when she said she loved me.

Some of 'em even cried!

Is it possible these women consider me a decent man even though I dreamed about and kissed another woman outside my marriage?

The worst part for Gentry comes when John Boone testifies he heard us talkin' about how Gentry's derringer appeared to be missin' a bullet. He also repeated what Gentry said about lookin' through the window was Daisy and Ezra's word against hers. And finally, he said she was reluctant to answer my question about lookin' through the window and said, "Why? So you can put me in *jail?* So you can watch them *hang* me?"

Them words caused everyone in the room to gasp.

Now, it's Gentry's turn in one of the chairs on either side of Margaret. After promisin' to tell the truth, she admits she lied to Daisy and Ezra Leek about not lookin' in the window, and Margaret makes her tell everyone what she saw. Even though they already knew, hearin' her say it makes her look guilty.

Margaret asks, "Were you, in fact, missing a bullet?"

Gentry answers, "Yes."

"Do you have an explanation for where it went?"

"No."

Someone yells, "*I do!* It went into Penelope's *chest!*"

The whole room comes alive with angry voices. Someone yells "Hang her!"

That type a' talk don't gain any followers, but as I look around the room it's pretty clear everyone thinks she's guilty.

Margaret asks why there are currently two bullets in her gun and she says she was afraid people would think she shot Penelope 'cause she'd been missin' a bullet. So she replaced it after we went home.

Margaret says, "Sheriff Love has asked to represent Gentry in these proceedings, so I'll let him have his say."

I stand and say, "I'll ask Enorma Suiters to come forward."

There are lots of reasons for the catcalls as Enorma makes her way to the front of the room, passes Gentry, and sits in the other chair beside Margaret. For one thing, there's her bosoms, which ain't like any you ever seen or heard about, and are famous throughout the county. It's one of— well, *two* of—the reasons she came in third *and fourth!*—in the beauty contest. Then there's her married name: Enorma Suiters, which sounds a lot like enormous hooters. And that's just her married name! Before gettin' hitched, her name was Enorma Stitz! So there's that. And of course, small towns bein' what they are, everyone knows about the time she stripped naked in front of me and tried to claim I was her lover. And now she lives next door to us, on account of I didn't know she and Benjamin Suiters were married when he offered to buy the land.

The main reason everyone's interested in hearin' what Enorma's got to say is they know she and Gentry don't like each other. So the fact I'm callin' her as a witness has got the whole room in a tizzy.

After Enorma agrees to tell the truth, I ask, "Have you ever asked Gentry if you could use her derringer?"

"Several times," she says.

"When's the last time you asked her?"

"Five or six days ago."

"And did she let you borrow her derringer?"

"No."

"Do you know why?"

"I do."

"Would you tell us?"

"She's a bitch!"

Everyone laughs.

Gentry grits her teeth.

Enorma sees her and says, "What're you gonna do, *shoot* me?"

John Boone rolls his eyes.

Margaret, lookin' concerned, asks, "Emmett, are you sure this is your witness?"

I say, "Enorma, you agreed to tell the truth."

"I *am* tellin' the truth!" she says. "Gentry—your wife—is a bitch."

More laughter.

I say, "What reason did Gentry give you for not lettin' you use her gun?"

"She claimed it was broken."

"Did she ever give you any other reasons?"

"No."

"Did she say *how* it was broken?"

"She said it wouldn't fire."

I notice people straighten' up in their seats, includin' John Boone, and Margaret, who holds up Gentry's gun and says, "Is this the derringer you asked to borrow?"

Enorma nods.

I say, "Margaret, have you inspected Gentry's derringer?"

She gives it a close look and says, "I don't know much about guns, but it looks okay to me."

"Would you cock it?"

"Why?"

"Please. Just cock it and see if it feels funny to you."

She cocks it. Says, "I'm sorry Emmett, but it feels fine to me. Anything else?"

"Yes. I'd like you to point it at me and shoot."

"That's not going to happen."

I ain't scared about gettin' shot, 'cause Scarlett already told me Gentry's gun can't shoot me, and I believe her. I tell

Margaret, "Gentry's life's on the line. I aim to prove her gun won't fire."

"We can do that by shooting at the floor."

"It's not the same."

"Why not?"

"Just shoot me. *Please.*"

"I will not. And if this is all you've got I suppose it's time to make my ruling."

"*I'll* shoot him," Gentry says.

"Excuse me?"

I notice Margaret is still holding the cocked gun. I yell, "Margaret!" then quick-draw my sidearm and aim it at her. She's so startled, she pulls the trigger, and hears a click. She cocks the other hammer, fires, and hears another click.

I holster my gun before anyone else in the room decides to shoot me. Then say, "As Gentry explained to Enorma, her gun won't shoot."

Everyone gets excited again, but for all the opposite reasons.

Margaret fiddles with Gentry's derringer a minute, then fires a shot into the floor and everyone shuts up except for John Boone, who says, "That's the best example I ever saw of shooting a hole in someone's case."

Gentry and I exchange looks of helplessness, even as the side door opens and two females enter. One of 'em says, "Margaret, *I'd* like to ask a couple of questions."

Gentry's eyes light up.

Mine do too!

It's Rose!

CHAPTER 41

WITH SCARLETT BY her side, Rose walks to the front of the room. Scarlett runs to Gentry and gives her a big hug. Then runs to me. Rose says, "Emmett, do I have your permission to continue on your behalf?"

"You sure as hell do!" I say, with no idea what she has in mind.

Rose walks over to Enorma, and says, "I think we can excuse Miss Titts from offering any further testimony."

Everyone laughs except Margaret and Enorma, though Margaret's strugglin' not to as she sees Enorma huffin' and puffin' over bein' made sport of. Then Rose tilts her head and says, "On second thought, I have a very important question for you, Enorma."

Enorma sits back down and says, "What?"

"Did you appear in the beauty contest on Sunday?"

"Yes."

"And how did you place?"

"Third and fourth."

Everyone laughs.

"And who beat you?"

"Ma'am?"

"I'm referring to the contest."

She points to Gentry. "Her and Penelope."

"And how did that make you feel?"

"I didn't really care one way or the other."

"Really? Because according to the people I spoke to, you were quite upset. You were cursing and kicking and complaining to your husband."

"So what if I was?"

"In a moment I'm going to call an eye witness who will testify she saw you picking through Gentry's dress at the *Lucky Spur*."

"What dress?"

"The one she changed out of before putting on the nicer one she wore for the contest."

Enorma's face turns a bright shade of red.

Rose says, "Do you want to tell Margaret what you did, or should I?"

"Tell her whatever you want."

Rose says, "Very well. Margaret? One of Gentry's employees caught Enorma going through the inside pockets of Gentry's dress while Gentry was in the final stages of the contest."

Margaret looks at her. "Is that true?"

Enorma says, "Maybe."

Rose says, "She was seen holding Gentry's gun."

Enorma says, "I was only checking to make sure she was telling the truth about it being broken."

"And did you remove any bullets?"

"I removed *both* of them," she says, proudly.

"And do you own a derringer?" Rose says.

"You know I don't."

"That's right," Rose says. "Because if you *did* own a derringer, you wouldn't ask to borrow Gentry's."

Margaret says, "What's your point, Rose?"

"I'll get to it quickly. "Enorma? What did you do with the bullets?"

"Threw them away."

"Both of them?"

"Yes."

"You promised to tell the truth."

"I *am!*"

Rose fixes her gaze on Enorma such that Enorma cries out, "I kept one of them."

"Where is it now?"

"In my house. In a drawer. In my bedroom."

"And what happened to the other bullet?"

"I don't know."

Rose says, "I'd like to excuse Enorma, and call Jamie Birdwhistle to testify."

Jamie takes Enorma's place in the chair and promises to tell the truth. Rose asks where she works, and Jamie says at the *Spur*. Then Rose says, "Out of anger, and seeking to play a prank on Gentry, Enorma decided to steal both bullets from Gentry's derringer. But Jamie, hearing a sound coming from Gentry's room, knocked and entered. She felt justified entering Gentry's private quarters because she knew neither Emmett nor Gentry could be in the room, since they were at the jail as judge and contestant in the beauty contest. Is everything I've said correct, Jamie?"

"Yes ma'am," Jamie says.

"Tell Margaret what happened next."

"After I opened the door to Miss Gentry's room?"

Rose nods.

Jamie says, "The big-titted girl jumped to her feet, dropped Miss Gentry's gun on the bed, and rushed out."

"Did she say anything to you?"

"She said, 'Don't say a word about this to anyone! I'm *supposed* to be here!'"

"After she left, what did you do?"

"Checked to make sure she didn't take nothin'."

"And did she?"

"I weren't sure."

"Did she take Gentry's derringer?"

"No ma'am."

"Besides the gun, what else did you find on the bed?"

"Gentry's dress and undergarments."

"Anything else?"

"A bullet."

"*One* bullet?"

"Yes, ma'am."

"How do you suppose it got there?"

"I reckon she dropped it when she dropped the gun."

"And what did you do with that bullet, Jamie?"

"Put it back in her gun."

"And did you tell Miss Gentry any of this?"

"No ma'am."

"Why not?"

"I was afraid I'd get in trouble."

"Why?"

"I didn't know if the big-titted girl was supposed to be there or not. I figured to keep my mouth shut and hope no one found out."

Rose says, "Not to state the obvious, but that explains how Gentry had but one bullet in her derringer, and why she had no knowledge of what happened to the other bullet. What I'm saying, Gentry couldn't possibly have shot Penelope."

"Then who did?"

"May I call someone else to testify?"

"By all means."

"Good. In that case, I'd like to call...."

CHAPTER 42

"OLIVER WAY," ROSE SAYS.

The crowd murmurs as Oliver makes his way to the front of the room. After agreein' to tell the truth Rose asks him, "Where were you the night your wife was shot?"

"Nowhere near the sheriff's office."

"You can do better than that, Oliver. Try again."

Rose closes her eyes, waitin' for him to speak. While she does, I notice Oliver's hands start twitchin' and his left eye squints like somethin' painful's stuck in it. He finally says, "I was at Miss Gilmore's house."

The crowd gasps. Most are lookin' around the room, searchin' for Miss Gilmore, to see her reaction.

Rose says, "Are you referring to *Jean* Gilmore, the local schoolteacher?"

"Yes."

"And was she there?"

"Yes."

"Let me rephrase the question. When you first arrived at Miss Gilmore's house, was she there?"

"No."

"But you entered her house anyway?"

He nods.

A number of wide-eyed women in the room cover their mouths, as if tryin' to imagine what he might say next.

Rose says, "What's your relationship with Miss Gilmore?"

At first he says nothin', but after twitchin' violently for ten seconds he grits his teeth and says, "We're lovers."

The crowd gasps again.

"By lovers, you mean...you fornicate with her, correct?"

"Yes."

"How many times a week?"

"That's none of your business."

"Perhaps not. But it's relevant."

"What are you talking about?"

"Do you know if Miss Gilmore happens to own a derringer?"

More twitchin', more squintin', then, "She does."

"And when she finally arrived home just after nine o'clock and found you there did she tell you she fired a shot moments earlier?"

"How could you possibly *know* that?"

"Is that a yes?"

He nods.

"Did she happen to mention she killed your wife, Penelope Way?"

The crowd erupts as Oliver shouts, "No! She did *not*! She said she shot a snake."

The crowd quiets down. Rose said, "She called your wife a *snake*?"

CHAPTER 43

AFTER FINISHING WITH Oliver, Rose calls on Jean Gilmore to testify. Miss Gilmore says very little, but admits shooting her derringer on the night Penelope was killed. Further questioning reveals she shot her "snake" at the exact time Penelope was killed. When Rose asked, "Is Penelope the snake you're referring to?" Miss Gilmore said, "Penelope was a snake all right. She got what she deserved."

Rose studies her carefully before sayin', "You haven't exactly admitted shooting Penelope Way, so I'll give you another chance to tell the truth. Did you in fact shoot her to death this past Sunday night?"

"I suppose I did."

Rose turns to Margaret. "Is that good enough for you?"

"It is. I hereby rule there's sufficient evidence to arrest Jean Gilmore for the murder of Penelope Way. Miss Gilmore will remain in custody in the sheriff's jail until such time as a judge sees fit to hold a proper trial. I further rule that all charges against Gentry Love are hereby dropped, with apologies on behalf of the entire community for doubting her, and for the inconvenience we've caused. I further rule that Emmett Love pay full restitution in the amount of $10 to Louis Hinkle—"

"—What the *hell?*" I say.

"—for fouling the floorboards of Mr. Hinkle's wagon," she says, "And another $40, should Mr. Hinkle decide to sell his fouled wagon to Sheriff Love."

"I'll sell it!" Louis says.

"Sorry, Emmett," Margaret says, "but this came up last night and I may as well rule on all matters at the same time." She smiles and says, "I further rule that Enorma Suiters shall be held accountable for the crime of illegal trespass, and the attempted theft of two bullets, the actual theft of a single bullet, and hereby order her to return the bullet in question to Gentry Love immediately, and to perform four hours of community service in the form of scrubbing the floorboards of the wagon Sheriff Love is about to acquire."

CHAPTER 44

Two Weeks Later...

1. MISS GILMORE'S ARREST has turned my jail into
   a complete madhouse. Bein' that she's the only
   school teacher in the county, the community voted
   to continue payin' her to teach the kids, even though
   the only place she can do that is from her jail cell,
   which means for six hours a day, five days a week,
   there are up to nine kids in the jail room bein'
   taught through jail bars.

2. Meanwhile, the dentistry supplies John Boone ordered before comin' to Dodge have finally arrived.
   Normally I'd put 'em in storage till after his trial, but
   since the county needs a dentist so badly, I'm

allowin' Boone to treat dental patients from his jail cell. And yes, he's still seein' legal clients as well.

3. You won't be surprised to learn that Boone and Miss Gilmore have become romantically involved. She hadn't been there three days when I caught 'em fuckin' through the bars that divide their cells, which is possible if she ain't facin' him, if you understand my meanin'. Lusty as she is, I've taught myself to knock on the jailhouse door and count to ten before openin' it.

4. I taught myself to check for snakes on Sundays when escortin' Miss Gilmore to the outhouse, so Scarlett's prophecy about dyin' on a Tuesday from gettin' bit by a shithouse snake on a Sunday won't come true on my watch.

5. Gentry and I had to scold Scarlett for puttin' a love spell on me that took hold whenever I saw or thought about Penelope.

"Why'd you do it?" I asked my daughter.

"Me and Rose were practicing spells," she said.

"Why'd you put one on *me*?"

"I was thinking about you at the time Rose challenged me."

"Why'd you pick Penelope?"

"I heard Mama say Penelope liked you, and I knew she was sad, and only had a week to live. She was a nice lady and

I thought if you fornicated with her it would make her happy."

I had to explain that fornicatin' ain't about makin' people happy.

"It makes *you* happy."

"Well...."

"It made Mr. Way and Miss Gilmore happy."

"Uh...."

"It makes Miss Gilmore and Mr. Boone happy."

"What do you know about *that?*"

"It's common knowledge fornicating makes people happy, as long as they're not fighting when they do it. You know why it makes people happy?"

"Why?"

"Because it *feels* good!"

She laughs harder when she sees my expression, and even harder when I holler "Bite your tongue, young lady! You don't know anything about that!"

After she calmed down I asked, "Did you put a love spell on *Penelope?*"

"I didn't have to. She always liked you."

I don't know why them words made me feel better, but they did. Which brings up a touchy subject:

6. Despite all I said about believin' Gentry, I ain't positive she didn't kill Penelope. I know Miss Gilmore confessed, but Rose has a witchy way about her, and felt responsible for lettin' Scarlett put a love spell on me that nearly destroyed my marriage. It's possible Rose made certain things happen to make Gentry

appear innocent. I asked her why she let Scarlett put the spell on me in the first place, and she said she didn't think Scarlett was mature enough to cast such a heavy a spell over such a far distance.

Though Gentry denied shootin' Penelope, I'm well acquainted with her jealous streak. She threatened to kill Enorma for disrobin' in front of me, and she definitely meant it. But a bigger reason I doubt her is because when Gentry handed her gun to me the night Penelope got shot, the barrel was as warm as any gun that might have been fired five minutes earlier.

All these things don't amount to proof, but they continued to nag at me because as a lawman, it didn't sit right that (a) my wife may have killed a woman for havin' a crush on me; and (b) Miss Gilmore shouldn't have to sit in jail or be tried and possibly hanged for a crime she may not have committed.

But them concerns left me last Sunday when Scarlett announced, "It's a good thing Miss Gilmore is still in jail."

"Why's that?" I asked.

"Today's the day she was supposed to get snakebit. But instead, she's found true love. Also...."

"What?"

"In the spring, she'll be Mrs. Boone. Then she'll go free."

"How's that possible?" She confessed to killin' Penelope!"

"The real killer will confess."

"Who's the real killer?"

"Oliver Way, of course!"

"If that's true, why did Miss Gilmore confess?"

"I made her."

"*You?*"

"I wanted to protect her and help her find true love."

"I thought you hated her."

"I did. But Rose challenged me to do something nice for someone I hated."

EPILOGUE

IT'S THE MIDDLE of winter, coldest day I ever lived through, though the day ain't over yet. Rose and Scarlett are with us, and likely savin' our lives, since the wood we're burnin' in the fireplace from Louis's wagon wouldn't normally be enough to make our house as warm as it is.

I have no idea what the rest of the town is doin' to stay warm, but Rose says she and Scarlett are helpin' out, whatever that means.

"This has to be the coldest day in the history of Kansas!" I say.

"Actually, it *is*," Rose says. "In the next 40 years only one day will be colder, and only by one degree."

"What day is that?"

"February 13, 1905."

"How cold will that one be?"

"Forty below zero."

"Well, I ain't likely to see that one, but Scarlett probably will."

"Shall I think of you on that day, Papa?" she says.

"Please do." Then I think to ask, "Does that mean we're gonna survive today?"

"Of course we will," Scarlett says. "We're burning magic wood."

I wouldn't call Louis's wagon magic wood, but thanks to Enorma's hard work, most of the floorboards were scrubbed clean enough to use for firewood. Still, Gentry and I are bundled up like beavers, and it's only by accident I happen to look out the window and see somethin' that don't seem possible: someone's trudgin' through the snow, headin' toward our house.

"What in the *world?*"

I open the door and nearly drop dead when I see who walks in:

It's old Hopeful Harold, from Rolla and Springfield, and he's smilin' fit to bust.

Gentry gives him a double look, like she's just seen a ghost. She squeals with delight and runs across the room to greet him. "*Harold?* Oh my *God!* I heard you were *dead!*"

"Who told you that?"

"Some traveler from Springfield."

"He must've been talkin' about the *other* old Harold, the one who died at the age of ninety-eight." He winks at Gentry and says, "I hope you don't mind I told the other Harold all about us before he passed."

Gentry lowers her eyes and smiles.

I say, "How old *are* you, Harold?"

"A hundred and one."

"How far'd you walk in all this snow?"

"Only half a mile. I spent the night in Dodge, at the hotel."

I shake my head in disbelief. I know strong young men who'd have problems walkin' that far in this type a' weather. I ain't sure I could do it myself.

We introduce him to Rose and Scarlett, who quickly excuse themselves to Scarlett's room and close the door, leavin' the three of us to stand there, lookin' at each other, till I give Gentry a secret wink and say, "What brings you here, Harold?"

He looks me straight in the eye and says, "Last time we spoke you said it'd be a cold day before you'd allow me to poke Gentry. Well, it *is*, and I'm here."

He looks at Gentry and says, "How about it?"

For a minute somethin' passes over my wife's eyes, some sort a' look that appears to be a mixture of deep sadness and great affection. Just as I think she might actually say yes, she kisses his cheek and says, "Not today, Harold."

"What about tomorrow?" he says.

She winks and says, "Ask me then, my darling, 'cause you never know!"

Author's Note

SOMETIMES TRUTH IS stranger than fiction.

It might seem far-fetched that Emmett would dig up Eli's body and transport it all the way to Wichita after failing to understand the Writ of Habeas Corpus, but misinterpreting legal documents was actually quite common in the old west.

In the late 1880's an Indian named Nah-diez-az was serving a life term in the Menard, Illinois Penitentiary, which, along with the Ohio Penitentiary, was one of two prisons under contract to the federal government. When a group called the Indian Rights Association filed a case on behalf of the Indians in both prisons, the Supreme Court issued a writ of habeas corpus that was misinterpreted by prison officials as a pardon. The result being that Nah-diez-az and ten other Indians were set free.

Personal Message from John Locke:

I LOVE WRITING books! But what I love even more is hearing from readers. If you enjoyed this or any of my other books it would mean the world to me if you'd take a moment to send a short email to introduce yourself and say hi.

I personally respond to my readers.

I would also love to put you on my mailing list so you can receive savings of up to 67% on eBooks immediately after publication. You'll also receive updates and have an opportunity to participate in contests and drawings.

Please visit my website,
http://www.DonovanCreed.com,
so I can personally thank you for trying my books.

John Locke

New York Times Best Selling Author

8th Member of the Kindle Million Sales Club
(which includes James Patterson, George R.R. Martin, and Lee Child)

John Locke had 4 of the top 10 eBooks on
Amazon/Kindle at the same time, including #1 and #2!

...Had 6 of the top 20 books <u>at the same time</u>!

...Had 8 books in the top 43 <u>at the same time</u>!

...Has written 27 books in five years in <u>six separate genres</u>,
<u>All best-sellers</u>!

...Has been published throughout the world in numerous languages
by the world's most prestigious publishing houses!

...Winner, Second Act Magazine's Story of the Year!

...Named by Time Magazine as one of the "Stars of the DIY-
Publishing Era"

Wall Street Journal: "John Locke (is) transforming
the 'book' business"

Donovan Creed Series:
Lethal People
Lethal Experiment
Saving Rachel
Now & Then
Wish List
A Girl Like You
Vegas Moon
The Love You Crave
Maybe
Callie's Last Dance
Because We Can!
This Means War!

Emmett Love Series:
Follow the Stone
Don't Poke the Bear
Emmett & Gentry
Goodbye, Enorma
Rag Soup

Dani Ripper Series:
Call Me
Promise You Won't Tell?
Teacher, Teacher

Dr. Gideon Box Series:
Bad Doctor
Box
Outside the Box

Other:
Kill Jill
Casting Call

Young Adult
A Kiss for Luck (Kindle Only)

Non-Fiction:
How I Sold 1 Million eBooks in 5 Months!

www.ingramcontent.com/pod-product-compliance
Lightning Source LLC
Chambersburg PA
CBHW070548130626
46556CB00001B/60